A Dance for Three

A Dance for Three

LOUISE PLUMMER

DELACORTE PRESS

Published by
Delacorte Press
an imprint of Random House Children's Books
a division of Random House, Inc.
1540 Broadway
New York, New York 10036

Copyright © 2000 by Louise Plummer

Library of Congress Cataloging-in-Publication Data
Plummer, Louise.
   A dance for three / Louise Plummer.
      p.   cm.
   Summary: When fifteen-year-old Hannah becomes pregnant and her rich,
popular boyfriend claims he is not responsible, she is forced to face some hard
facts about her life.
   ISBN 0-385-32511-8
   [1. Pregnancy Fiction.   2. Mental illness Fiction.   3. Family problems
Fiction.   4. Mothers and daughters Fiction.]   I. Title.
PZ7.P734Dan   2000
[Fic]—dc21   99-30877
                                                                 CIP

The text of this book is set in 12-point Sabon.
Book design by Debora Smith
Manufactured in the United States of America
March 2000
10   9   8   7   6   5   4   3   2   1

To Charles and Erica

Seal Lullaby

BY RUDYARD KIPLING

Oh! hush thee, my baby, the night is behind us,
And black are the waters that sparkled so green.
The moon, o'er the combers, looks downward to find us
At rest in the hollows that rustle between.
Where billow meets billow, there soft be thy pillow;
Ah, weary wee flipperling, curl at thy ease!
The storm shall not wake thee, nor shark overtake thee,
Asleep in the arms of the slow-swinging seas.

PART I
Hannah Speaks

M*ilo wasn't the first boy to kiss me but he was the first one to bite me. I said "Ouch," and he said, "Let me lick it better." It was when his mouth was on my shoulder and his hands tugged my camisole down that I knew I would go all the way with him. I would lose my virginity with Milo in the back of his Toyota 4Runner parked above the cemetery with the lights of Salt Lake City below. Not that we were looking. I kissed him fiercely. Too fiercely. He said, "Slow down; it's better slow."*

Did I do it because I loved him or because he was so persuasive? Did I do it because I knew Mama wouldn't approve? Did I want a baby? Or maybe it was the madness taking hold inside me.

Madness runs in families, and, like baldness, skips generations. Mama told me this, secure in the knowledge that she is the skipped generation. "You're more like your grandma Satterfield." She looks at my stomach when she talks to me.

When I steal the roses, I lean over the bush pretending to smell and admire the blooms. Daddy's shirt arches out from my body and hides the plucking motion. Rose and stem fall into the canvas Earth bag I carry. I steal roses from everyone up and down our block. My rule is not to leave the block. It's more exciting to risk being caught and humiliated by close neighbors.

I don't have to steal. Our yard has dozens of rosebushes and Mama doesn't care if I cut them. In fact, she thinks all those roses hanging upside down, drying out in my bedroom, are from our yard. "It's Hannah's hobby," she tells people who come to visit, and she shows them the bouquet of dried roses in the brass vase by the fireplace. "Aren't they lovely?"

Her friends admire that arrangement of stolen roses. I would love to say, "I stole all of them," and watch Mama's surprised face, watch her stammer excuses to the guests.

Am I awful?

Now I am cutting a yellow Eclipse, I think, although I sometimes confuse them with Oregolds. And I am humming a lullaby about baby seals, a song my daddy taught me. I hum, because I read that babies can hear their mothers' voices from inside the womb. It's the earliest bonding you can do, I guess. I have missed my period two months in a row, and I am singing lullabies just in case somebody's listening.

The yellow rose falls into the bag. It is the second rose I've cut from Mrs. Keddington's yard. She's a safe bet, because she sleeps late and it's early right now. There's no thrill in safety, though, and I move on to Rosa Benson's yard. She never sleeps. It's heartthrobbing exciting to steal from her. Her voice alone can beat you up. I lean over and smell a few roses on the south side of her house, where she can see me from either the living room or kitchen windows. I can feel her eyes and I don't cut anything. Instead I pick up a candy wrapper on the sidewalk and throw it in the bag. I have my virtues.

I walk along the front of Rosa Benson's house until I am on the north corner. It's the blind-spot side of her house. No windows anywhere. She can't see me from the front window; it's set back too far. She'd have to come out on her porch to see me snipping one of her Miss All-American Beauties.

"Hannah Ziebarth, are you stealing my roses?" She *is* on the porch, leaning out over the metal railing.

I look up the steep slope of the lawn at her and am zinged by the sun coming up behind her house.

"No, ma'am. I am not. I just picked up this candy wrapper off your lawn." I show her. "Mama sent me out to clean up the block."

She's unsure now. It sounds like the sort of wacky thing my mama might do. We both know this. I screw my face into perfect innocence. "You wanna see?" I hold the canvas bag toward her.

She heaves her flat chest. She's had both breasts cut off. No one on our block is whole. Mrs. Keddington had a kidney removed. Mrs. de Groot had her spleen cut out after a car accident. Mrs. Goodrow, our neighbor to the south, has lost her mind, and Mr. Knight, the only man on our block, had his leg blown off in the Vietnam War. It made him bitter, and that's why he is ruining our neighborhood by moving dirt around with his yellow backhoe and letting all the rental property he owns go straight to the dogs. I'm quoting Mama.

"I know exactly what's in that bag," Rosa Benson says. "A whole bunch of other people's roses and a few scraps of paper. Don't steal my roses, Hannah. I'm warning you."

"I won't," I say, and I wave real friendly like and she looks like her head's going to explode right off her neck, because she knows the truth and she knows that I know the truth, but I don't care and she does. Even though I'm only fifteen, I know that she who cares least has the most power, so I win.

I walk up toward Mr. Knight's.

When I have this baby—if there is a baby—I'm moving off McClelland Street forever. I'm moving to a place where the sidewalks are smooth and not cracked and crooked, where there are young kids like me and not a lot of old geezers with their body parts cut out. A place of new houses, with swimming pools, aquamarine rectangles in the sun. I'll move in with Milo. He'd want that.

I pick all the blooms off Mr. Knight's Peace Rose bush. I'm not even careful, because I can hear the backhoe sputtering behind the house across the street. Mr. Knight is moving dirt again.

Renters don't count on our block. So when I say no

one is whole on our block, I'm referring to the home-owners. I don't know that much about the renters, except that Mama says they're just transients, which I always thought meant homeless, but I guess not. The houses in our neighborhood are easy to rent, because they're convenient to both downtown and the university.

Mama is a homeowner, of course. She owns our brick bungalow clear, because Daddy's insurance paid for it when he died two years ago. He died of a burp. I'm not kidding. He burped after a Saturday-night dinner and died seven minutes later. Death by asphyxiation: the valve in his epiglottis failed to close again after a slight regurgitation, and food got into his windpipe, then into his lungs, and suffocated him. He went fast. Nobody knew what happened. Not him. Not us. I dream all the time that he comes back, I want it so much. Come back, Daddy, and let Mama and me be the people we were before you went away. Before we forget what those people were like.

Every time I burp now, I wait to die.

I begin to cross the street, intending to work the other side. Every yard on our block has roses, although some of them don't dry well. Climbers don't, so I don't even bother with them. I feel a commotion. And sure enough when I turn, I see Mrs. Goodrow, still in her night-gown, standing on the sidewalk in front of her house gesturing about god only knows what. I turn back and head toward her. When she sees me, she stumbles in my direction and we meet in front of my house. "Oh, Hannah," she says, taking my hands, "all the drainpipes are filled with leaves, and I'm afraid I'm going to have water running into the basement again." Her head goes down. She gasps hard like she's just emerged from water. "Would you ask your dad to come over and fix them? I wouldn't ask, but I'm so afraid of flooding the basement again—" Her basement flooded once thirty years ago. "Do you think he would?" The anxiety in her voice is much greater than the perceived problem. It hasn't rained for weeks.

"I'm sure he'll do it," I say. "But you better change, you wouldn't want him to see you in your nightgown, would you?"

She notices the nightgown for the first time. "Oh, my, what could I be thinking, coming outside in my night-gown?" She covers her mouth with trembling fingers and laughs underneath them. "Your dad would think I've lost my mind if he saw me like this."

Yes, I think he would. I smile and bob my head up and down like a ventriloquist's dummy. It is summer vacation, the middle of June, and I should not have to deal with these ironies. I take Mrs. Goodrow's arm and lead her to her house, walk her up the steps of the slope and onto her front porch, where she pats my hand gratefully. "You're such a good girl, Hannah," she says, her yellow teeth bared. Her white hair has mostly lost its permanent and spikes out in disarray from her head. She has been old since I have known her, but she has only been out of her mind a couple of years. If the old Mrs. Goodrow could see herself now, she'd put in a call to Dr. Kevorkian.

Sometimes when I think of the difference between

myself now and myself before Daddy died, I want to call Dr. Death myself. I didn't even have periods two years ago, and now I'm probably pregnant. When did I forget how to be a child?

When Mrs. Goodrow is safely in her house, I go home, next door, with my roses—about two dozen of them. "Hello, it's just me," I cry, opening the back door.

I can hear Mama's low voice on the phone in her bedroom but cannot distinguish words. She could be talking to the doctor. He said he would call first thing in the morning. Instinctively I look out the window to the east bench where Milo lives. What is he doing now? Words of the "Seal Lullaby" float into my head: "Ah, weary wee flipperling, curl at thy ease—" I think of Daddy. He wrote music to those words just for me. A small panic rises in my throat and I swallow several times.

I'm hungry. I should make something to eat. I pull out the Bisquick, eggs, and milk. I plug in the electric frying pan. Mama is mostly silent now, except for a word now and then. Is she crying?

I would rather not be thinking of Milo and me entangled in the back of his 4Runner, but I can't stop.

I measure ingredients haphazardly. It doesn't matter. Bisquick is one of those ingenious products that turns into something edible no matter what you do to it.

I can no longer hear Mama's voice. Her hands are on my shoulders, and I am bent over the pancake mix. "Hannah." There are tears in her voice, which I hate.

I don't turn around. "What'd he say?" The pancake batter needs more milk.

"He says you're pregnant." She rests her head on my shoulder, weeping. "What are we going to do? I don't know what to do. I never expected my life to be like this, Hannah."

"I didn't either," I say. "We'd better eat breakfast."

She nods and sits at the table and waits like an invalid. I pour the batter into the hot pan, rush plates and utensils to the table, flip the pancakes, and pour milk into the glasses. When I place a stack of pancakes on her plate she says, "You forgot to put down place mats and napkins. I hate eating straight off the table like this. It makes me feel like an animal." She begins weeping again.

"Sorry, I was distracted." I pull two plaid yellow cotton place mats and matching napkins out of a drawer and quickly arrange them under the dinnerware. When I get back to take my pancakes out of the pan, they are too brown.

"You know it's in times of crisis that details matter most. If you allow yourself to become slovenly, your whole life falls apart." She winces at the bottle of Aunt Jemima syrup sitting on the table. I know she would like me to have put it in a pitcher and heated it in the microwave. Her attention to detail does not include her appearance. She wears baggy pants and a shirt with a frayed collar.

I take several bites of burned pancakes but my stomach revolts. The syrup is too sweet, too thick. I breathe slowly, waiting for the nausea to subside.

Mama puts her fork down. "I'm sorry, Hannah." Her voice trembles again. "You do so much. I wish I could do it, but I can't. I don't know why, but I just can't. I thought about cooking you a breakfast this morning, but I couldn't remember how. Honestly, I can't remember how to fix anything."

I hate it when she cries. She expects me to soothe her, like I'm *her* mother. It's not like I don't have my hands full already. "It's okay," I say. "Besides, you take good care of your plants. We have a whole miniature forest right here in the house." I'm good at making my voice sound jolly even when I'm irritated.

It brings her around. She nods happily. "Bonsai have saved my life. It's the one thing I can still do."

I tell her about Mrs. Goodrow. "She wanted Daddy to fix her drainpipes," I say.

"Did you tell her your daddy's dead?"

"Nope."

"Hannah! What'll she think when he doesn't show up?"

"I'm sure she's forgotten all about the drainpipes by now. She can't hold anything in her head longer than three minutes, if that long."

Mama is skeptical. "She's not that bad—"

"Besides," I say. "I've told her at least four times that he's dead and each time it's like the first time. She cries and asks about the funeral and the viewing and where we're going to bury him. I can't stand to go through that again."

"I suppose not." She pushes the last pancake out to the rim of the plate. "Well, I need to go back to my babies. Will you get me those two crab-apple plants out in back? I'm grafting them today." She pushes away from the table. "And the white mulberry and the orange jessamine need to go back outside for full sun." She kisses me and leaves me to run her outside errands.

Lots of people don't know that bonsai plants are meant to grow outside. Before Daddy died, Mama worked out on the back patio, where Daddy had constructed a long worktable. Against the house he built rows of shelves layered like bleachers for displaying the plants. She still worked out there for a short time after he died, but then one day—and I wasn't there, so I don't know exactly what happened—Mama had a huge panic attack out there. That's the doctor's term, not hers. She said someone was trying to strangle her and drag her to hell. That's just what it felt like, she said. She said she couldn't catch her breath, and her face became all paralyzed and tingly, and the sun turned black.

It was a sunny summer day she's talking about. I know, because Trilby and I were burying all her Barbie and Ken dolls out in her backyard, a block and a half up the hill from McClelland Street, and the sun did not darken. Trilby started her period that day and thought it was a mature act to bury the dolls. We stuck them in two old hatboxes and buried them near the iris bed where the dirt is loose, and we had no trouble shoveling a couple of holes.

Ever since that day when the devil tried to strangle Mama and drag her into hell, I have had to bring the bonsai from the stands on the back patio to the "solarium" in the front of the house, where Mama can work free of panic and return them to the backyard the next day. It's really not a solarium where she works on the bonsai. It's a small music room with one stretch of narrow windows near the ceiling and Daddy's old upright Steinway on the opposite wall. The piano is covered with pots of bonsai even over the covered keys. Because Daddy is the only one who played, it's become, in my mind, a grotesquely decorated coffin.

Today, when Mama learns I'm pregnant, she doesn't ask about Milo. What will Milo think? She doesn't ask what I'm going to do about the baby, if I'm scared. She doesn't say, What about high school? She doesn't say, You're not even old enough to drive yet. She doesn't ask, What can I do?

Actually she tells me what she wants me to know. She says she can't remember how to fix breakfast or anything else for that matter. The implication is clear: she can't take care of me either.

After breakfast I carry the mulberry and jessamine out to the backyard and set them down on a shelf, pick up a crab-apple plant, hold it high above my head, and bring it smashing down to the concrete patio. It sounds like a skull breaking open, painful and strangely satisfying. But seeing the bare roots separated from the dirt just makes me feel sad. While I gather the plant and dirt into another pot, I think surely I am insane.

You have to let the phone ring a million times at Milo's house. He has two sisters and two brothers, and they all think someone else should answer the phone. Or they're all in the swimming pool out in back, and they couldn't hear a phone no matter how long you let it ring. I don't know how long I've been hanging on to this phone practicing writing "Mrs. Milo Fabiano" on a pad next to the phone. "Hannah Fabiano." "Milo and Hannah Fabiano," and I'm about to hang up when I hear Mrs. Fabiano's voice.

"It's Hannah," I say, and I ask for Milo.

"Oh, Hannah, you sweet thing; how are you?"

Your son made me pregnant, thanks. But I really say, "I'm great. How was your trip to St. George?"

"Mostly it was hot. A hundred and five down there yesterday. I just stayed inside with the girls. The boys all went golfing. Milo, Roman, and their dad stayed over another day, but I expect them back early this afternoon." Suddenly her voice is muffled and I can hear her telling Rose not to tease the cat. "Sorry," she says when she returns. "The kids are going swimming. Why don't you come up and join them? You can have lunch with us. Milo should be back soon after that."

I've never been to Milo's house when he wasn't there, and this invitation seems strangely intimate. I don't know what to say.

Anyway, she says to remember to bring my suit and she'll be seeing me in a few minutes. I hang up the phone and look at it. Well, why shouldn't I go up there and be with the family, *my* new family? I'm having your grandchild, Mrs. Fabiano. What do you think of that?

I swallow several times, because I don't know what I think of it yet. I make a dried rose bouquet for Mrs.

Fabiano, which I tie with three narrow pastel ribbons, and put my suit and hairbrush in a canvas bag.

Mama is in the bonsai room, bent over her babies. "I'm going over to Milo's," I say. I hold up the canvas bag. "We're going swimming."

"What about lunch?" She has finished tying the knot and rubs her hands on her apron.

"I made you a sandwich. It's in a Baggie in the fridge. And there's potato chips left and a pudding cup. I'll get more groceries on the way home." I put on my jolly face.

"I don't really need anything. I'm just here alone. Not that I complain, because I don't. There are a lot of people lonelier than I am in the world. Are you taking the bus?" Mama pulls conversational switcharoos all the time, moving from cosmic loneliness to public transportation.

"Yes," I say, and usually that would be true, but this time I'm lying, because I've decided to drive from now on, even though I don't have a driver's license and I'm too young to get one. If I can be pregnant, I can drive. That's justice.

"Bye," I call on my way out the front door. Besides, what's the point of having a three-year-old Prizm sitting out in the garage? A perfectly good car that hasn't been driven for two years. A car with less than twenty thousand miles on it. A car Mama doesn't want to sell, because it was Daddy's. If you ask me, there's no point in it.

The garage is not attached to the house but is built

into the slope of the front yard on the street level. Mama can't see it from the window. Still, I look up at the house just to make sure she's not on the front porch. It would be the first time in a long time if she were.

There are two separate garage doors made of wood and in bad need of varnish. I open the right one as slowly as I can. It creaks, and I wait a little and then open it all the way. I yank off the dust cover protecting the car, wad it in a heap and throw it into a corner. The Prizm still shines as if Daddy just came back from the Wash n' Wax. My throat thickens. I try to breathe normally, and I am able to when the key I copied works in the lock. I get in the driver's side, where it takes me several seconds to find the ignition. I say a little prayer in case there's anyone still listening, and *voilà*, the engine turns over. I've learned to be grateful for small gifts. I back the car out slowly. I haven't had a lot of practice, but I do just fine. It's too bad no one's around to tell me what a good job I'm doing, but then I've gotten used to that too. When I get out of the car to close the garage door, I see that Mrs. Benson is sitting in that old webbed aluminum chair of hers on her front porch. The look on her face tells me that she is trying to remember what year I was born. I pull the garage door down, walk back to the car efficiently, and wave up at one of the living room windows of our house. Then I drive up the street as if I know what I'm doing. As Milo said when he was teaching me, "Any moron can drive."

The Fabianos live a couple of miles northeast of my

house, but it might as well be in another universe. Large two- and three-story brick houses with long windows line the streets along with eighty-year-old sycamore trees, whose heavy branches meet overhead to make a leafy shelter. The lawns and gardens are maintained by professional gardeners. Jaguars, Mercedes, and Saab convertibles are parked in driveways.

I park the Prizm a couple of blocks from Milo's house, because Mrs. Fabiano knows exactly how old I am. She knows I'll be sixteen on August 8. The thing is, she thinks teenagers shouldn't date until they're sixteen. Milo is almost seventeen, and because I'm fifteen, she won't let him date me. It's okay for us to be "good friends," so she's always inviting me up to the house, where there are tons of kids watching our every move. Milo says his mother is trying to control teen sexual activity with this rule. She's afraid of teen orgies catching on right here in the neighborhood. He tells me this when we are naked as new rabbits in his bed while his family is away.

"Her theory really works, don't you think?" He pulls me under the covers, and we break up laughing.

Of course she lets Milo come and get me and take me home. Sometimes it takes a long time to take me home. Like when we did it the first time, at the end of March, we took a detour via Eleventh Avenue above the cemetery there. Milo told her he was talking with my mama about bonsai. Bonsai, schmonzai.

Mrs. Fabiano greets me at the front door. "Hannah, I'm so glad to see you," she says. She has this gorgeous smile and moves forward to kiss each of my cheeks while at the same time—this seems so strange— she presses the palms of her hands against my shoulders as if pushing me away. As if I was the one who came forward to kiss her. Maybe that's the way sophisticated people do it. Kiss and push away. Very chichi.

"Thanks for inviting me," I say. I hand her the dried bouquet, which now, standing here under the portico, seems pretty cheap. Still I say, "I made them," in case she thinks I bought them at Pier 1 or something.

She holds them as if I've given her the crown jewels and tells me how wonderful I am and how she can't do anything with her hands, and even though I don't believe it, I'm grateful. Then she looks up and down the street. "How did you get here so fast?" She puts her arm through mine and draws me into the house.

"A neighbor drove me." I am sorry to have to lie, but why do adults have to sniff out every little deviation from the norm?

She lays the dried roses next to a vase on a side table with a marble top where they look really nice. I take an easier breath.

"I would have come to get you myself, except the house is filled with starving kids." She leads me to the kitchen, where Rose and Gina, the seven-year-old twins, are snarfing down bacon from a plate next to the electric frying pan.

Mrs. Fabiano moves the plate out of reach. "You little stinks," she says, "that was for sandwiches."

I think of the woman on our block, one of the renters, who calls her kids little shits. Little stinks is appealingly quaint.

"We only want bacon," Rose says.

"I'll make some more," I say.

"Can I help?" Gina tugs on my shorts.

"*May* I help," Mrs. Fabiano says.

"If you take your thumb out of your mouth," I say.

She releases her thumb with a popping noise and grins.

"Clever girl," I say.

"You're magic, Hannah," Mrs. Fabiano whispers. "You're the only one who can make her stop sucking her thumb."

Gina hears every word and says, "Make her live with us, Mom, so she can help me with my thumb." She holds up a withered, raw thumb.

"Good grief," I say, and fill the pan with bacon strips.

"She would be our big sister," Rose says. "Wouldn't you?"

"I guess. Don't get too close; you'll get a grease burn," I say, moving Gina's chair.

"Would you be Tony's older sister too?"

"Yes."

"And Roman's?"

"Yes, but only by a few months."

Mrs. Fabiano looks up from cutting tomatoes, her lips suppressing a smile.

"And Milo too. Would you be Milo's older sister?"

"No." I couldn't help laughing. "I'd be his younger sister. Milo's older than I am."

"I think Hannah would rather be Milo's friend," Mrs. Fabiano says, "than his sister—and vice versa."

Wife. Lover. I'd rather be those.

"She could still live with us," Rose says. "Do you want to?"

"Where would I sleep?" I ask. We are now assembling the BLTs.

"In our trundle bed." Gina spreads a grossly thick layer of mayonnaise onto white bread.

"Yeah!" Rose cheers. "In our room."

"I'd like that," I say.

"You'd fit right in." Mrs. Fabiano smiles. "Come on, we'll eat poolside."

Milo's room is upstairs with its own queen-size bed and its own bathroom and a closet the size of Mama's "solarium." I imagine my clothes in there next to his, my shoes next to his: His and Her Dr. Martens. I'd learn to do things like Mrs. Fabiano—have my nails "done," set the table with all those extra forks and spoons in the right place, and buy soap at Nordstrom's instead of the grocery store. I could be droll and say "you little stinks" to Gina and Rose to show them that they could eat all the bacon they wanted, because there is always more where that came from. I'd help around the house, and go grocery shopping, and change lightbulbs, and use "lie" and "lay" correctly. I could fit in. And when the baby came, she would fit in too. These were her relatives, after all. Milo's mother, with her tanned, waxed legs and faint cleavage, would be Grandma Fabiano.

Mama's home grafting crab-apple seedlings, barely

capable of getting her fixed lunch out of the refrigerator. The thought makes me choke.

"Are you all right? Hannah? Hannah dear?" Mrs. Fabiano's concerned face is near mine and she is slapping me on the back while I am gasping for air.

"Yes," I say, grabbing her arm. I don't want her hitting me on the back—it doesn't help. "Yes, I just got something stuck in my throat."

"But you haven't even taken a bite."

"I couldn't breathe," I say. I could tell her now how I get lumps in my throat suddenly and I start breathing hard. I could tell her. And she might say, "Oh that! I get that all the time. It's nothing." I'd be so relieved. But I can't tell her, because she's more likely to say, "I've never heard of such a thing," and look at me as if I'm insane. I couldn't stand that.

"Hey, Hannah, did you choke on some air?" Tony and his friends laugh from the pool.

"Yeah, the air is so rarefied where you are," I say.

They pretend to choke and float limply in the water as if they're dead. I smile at Mrs. Fabiano. "I'm fine," I say. "Really." To show her how fine I am, I take a huge bite out of my sandwich and gulp some lemonade.

This seems to work, because she turns her attentions to the twins, who are eating only potato chips. "You have to eat some tomato and lettuce too," she tells them. She turns back to me. "They're going to die of heart attacks at age eight; they eat only fat." She brushes hair off Rose's forehead. "Milo was the same way when he was their age, but now he at least eats rice." She smiles. "He *loves* rice!" I like it that she shares something about Milo with me, as if she recognizes that he and I are a potentially permanent couple, and that it is okay with her.

"Rice and Ho Hos," I say.

She laughs. "He does have a Ho Ho addiction. Pretty serious!" Her short hair swings when she moves her head back, and I wonder how she gets it so shiny. I want to ask her what she uses, but it seems too dumb. "Oh, I forgot to tell you," she says suddenly. She holds my bare arm to let me know that this is really something wonderful. "It's a good thing that Frank—Mr. Fabiano—stayed over with Milo and Roman, because they met this couple on the golf course. The man was an undergraduate at Harvard years ago and recruits in Utah for them. Can you believe it? Anyway, Frank told them that he got his M.B.A. there and that Milo was applying this fall, and Desmond—that was the man's name, Desmond Leighton—said he would do all he could to get Milo into Harvard." Her palms come together in not quite a clap. "As it turns out, his wife was a Chi Omega a few years after me: Kathy Habbeshaw. I remember her vaguely. I think she played the cello or something." Her eyebrows rise in a silent cheer. "Lucky for Milo to run into these people. Everything helps."

I nod and try to smile. "Very lucky," I say, and my breathing is not quite right again.

"You're going to pledge, aren't you, when you get to the U? Oh, I know it's a couple of years away, but you should start planning now—make contacts—I'll help, of course. You'd fit right in at Chi Omega."

"I'm going to Harvard too." I can hardly believe that

I've said this. But really it sort of pisses me off that it's a given that Milo will go to Harvard and that I'll stay here and join her precious Chi Omega. For the briefest moment, I dare to dislike her.

"Oh, I'm so creepy with my assumptions." It's an apology. "There's no reason why you shouldn't go to Harvard too. Forgive me for being so"—she searches—"so unforgivable." Her smile is wide and meant to warm me, and it does.

"It's okay," I say. "Even if I did get in, I probably couldn't afford it." What am I talking about? I'm pregnant. My grades aren't that great. I test badly. My dad is as dead as Napoleon. My mother is the bonsai queen. I can't breathe right.

Mrs. Fabiano has gotten up to help the twins into the pool. Even though they are good swimmers, she still makes them wear water wings, which makes Rose mad. "I'm not a baby," she says, but she jumps into the water.

Mrs. Fabiano takes off the swimsuit cover she's been wearing, sits back down, and spreads her pretty legs out in front of her. "Harvard *is* very expensive."

I am trying to breathe normally, but this conversation is making it difficult. I don't know why exactly.

"You know, my mother grew up right on your block." Her head rests on the back of the chair and her eyes are closed. "I knew she grew up on McClelland Street, but I didn't realize it was right on your very block, right there next to Judge Memorial." She meant the parochial school.

Was she trying to find another connection between us besides Milo?

"Yes, it's now Mrs. Keddington's house. Milo showed me." I swallow some lemonade, hoping the lumps in my throat will go down with it. "The neighborhood has changed a lot since your mother lived there." Let me count the ways. "A lot of the houses have been turned into rental units."

"Oh, but it's still pretty, I'm sure."

"Yes."

I'm in the pool playing submarine with the twins when Milo comes home. "Hey, Ziebarth," he yells. "I just tried to call you."

"I'm not home," I call back. The twins giggle.

"No, duh." He smiles widely, a smile that resembles his mother's, I now realize.

"Put on your suit and come in," I say.

He nods and disappears into the house.

Roman, his brother, comes to the open doorway for a moment and turns to go back in.

"Hi, Roman," I yell. "How was the golfing?"

He looks embarrassed to have been noticed. He nods even before he speaks. "Good," he says. "Real good."

"Come and join us!"

He turns as if looking for an excuse not to, or permission, or something. He's unbelievably shy. Milo says he's been that way since he lost the use of one eye in a hiking accident when he was ten.

"Get your suit," I prod.

"Okay." He says it so low I can hardly hear him. He was in English class with me last year, and we still don't talk any easier than before. It could be my fault. The dead eye wanders a little. I'm never sure which eye to look at. Maybe he senses this.

Soon Milo races from the house in his bathing suit and cannonballs into the pool, creating a wall of water that hits me and the twins directly. We scream, and he continues the attack by pushing water at us with the palms of his hands. The twins shove up against him and try to push him over. He picks up Gina and tosses her and repeats the action with Rose. They squeal and rush back at him for more. They are dark-haired, dark-eyed, all three of them. They are as Italian as their father. I heard Mrs. Fabiano, who is fair-skinned and blue-eyed, say once that if she hadn't been at their births, she wouldn't believe they were her children.

Milo's and my child will look Italian too. Milo's and my child. Milo. What will he think?

"Gina and Rose, time to get ready for violin lessons. Hurry out. Right now." Mrs. Fabiano stands between the French doors, one hand shading her eyes.

The twins groan and paddle for the stairs.

"There's lots of pop and fruit in the fridge, you two," Mrs. Fabiano cries.

When they are all in the house, Milo grabs me around the waist and says, "Let's do it here in the water."

"Milo, no. Someone could see us." I try to wriggle loose, but his grasp tightens. He kisses my shoulder.

"Let's do it floating." His leg curls around mine and he laughs.

"Geez. You're an idiot." But when the kiss comes, I open my mouth. He pulls my legs around his waist. I close my eyes. The water laps around our shoulders. "No one would see us," he whispers into my mouth.

I open my eyes and see a figure standing at the edge of the pool. "Roman!" It comes out forced, too bright.

Milo backs away and seems to tread water. "Hey, guy, make a little noise, will ya?"

"Sorry, I didn't mean to sneak up on you." He sits at the edge of the pool and slowly slides into the water. He looks more naked than most people in a bathing suit, too skinny, too stooped in the shoulders.

We sidestroke in a circle. Milo tells me that Roman shot par on the golf course that morning. "He kicked our butts," he says.

Roman smiles. "Somebody needs to," he says.

They begin to spar in the water. I feel left out and swim to the deep end and backstroke a couple of laps across the width of the pool. My head hits something—I think it is the side of the pool, but it's not. A hand comes down over my face and pushes me into the water and holds me down. I don't have time to take a good breath, and I panic and flail all my limbs uselessly. This isn't funny, I think. This isn't funny. I'm out of breath. God help me, I'm out of breath, and someone thinks it's funny. I thrash against a body. It's not just a hand holding me down anymore. Someone's sitting on my head and shoulders. It must be Roman. Milo's always saying what a stupid sense of humor he has. My lungs are empty and I know I will pass out, know I will die of a joke just like Daddy died of a burp. A big joke. People have to suppress grinning when you tell them. Daddy, help me.

Suddenly the weight on my head is gone and someone has grabbed my arm to help pull me up. I gasp for air and cough. The hand is still holding me. It is Roman's. He's holding on to the side of the pool, yelling over my head at Milo, who's treading water and grinning a few feet from me.

"It's not funny!" Roman's voice is hoarse.

"Oh, get a grip. She's all right. She wasn't down there more than a few seconds. You're all right, aren't you, Ziebarth?" Milo swims over and rubs my shoulder. I can't stop coughing.

"It was a lot longer than a few seconds, you friggin' sadist." Roman's face is red. One blood vessel throbs in his forehead.

"You learn that in those remedial classes you take?" Milo asks.

Roman lunges at him, and the two of them thrash in the water until I yell for them to stop. "Please, I'm all right, really," I tell Roman, who has blood streaming from his nose. "It's not worth this." I turn to Milo. "Really it isn't," I say.

Milo's jaw is set, his nostrils flared. "Get out of here," he says to Roman, who wipes his nose uselessly. The blood runs over his lips.

I feel like throwing up.

Roman climbs out of the pool. "Now you can kill her in peace," he says, and disappears into the house.

"I've got to go," I say, and turn away.

Milo catches my arm. "You mad?"

"I was out of breath."

"Come on, Ziebarth, you're a regular fish."

I swim to the shallow end and walk out of the pool.

"A fish with great legs," he says, following me. "Hey, Ziebarth." He swings me around. "Okay, I'm sorry. No, I'm morose. I beg your forgiveness." He looks at the house to see if his mother is anywhere around and then puts his arms around me and pulls me in tight. "Let me kiss it better."

He kisses me full on the lips. I don't open my mouth.

Meeting Milo was a fluke. We don't run in the same circles. He was junior-class vice president last year and played in all the very big-deal sports and was Mr. Very Big Deal himself at one of the dances. Mr. Touchdown or Mr. Catapult or Mr. Man-in-the-Moon. Who keeps track? Meanwhile, I sit in the orchestra playing second flute to Germaine Eggleston, who takes her first position very seriously and never turns the page of the music score we share, even if I, as second flutist, am playing sixteenth notes at a *presto* speed at the end of the page and she has measures full of rests—she still doesn't turn the page. "It's the job of the second chair to turn the pages," she tells me on the first day of class. She also tells me that she had a master class with flutist Phillipe LeCorday last summer in Paris, and he said she had the finest *embouchure* he'd ever seen. I just stare at her, although I should be genuflecting.

Still, despite these social differences, I meet Milo Fabiano on a mild but windy February day after school on the football field. Trilby and I often walk out of the auditorium, where the orchestra practices, and cut across the football field to the next block. That day, guys are playing a pickup game of soccer, and a pretty good-sized crowd stands along one side of the field. I recognize Mimi Manderino and Roman, who is in my English class. Trilby and I stand briefly on the edge of this group to watch the game.

Before I actually see Milo's face on the playing field, I see his flannel shirt. It is a blue-and-green plaid, unbuttoned in the front and worn over a white T-shirt. The wind gusts across the field, blows up the back of the shirt, which billows out from Milo's back and looks like a strange kite that might lift him right off the ground and float him away. I anticipate, mouth open, that the wind will carry him off, but soon the shirt flattens and I am aware of Milo kicking the ball in short strokes, his head and shoulders bent, his face determined. Two boys from the opposing team flank him, kicking uselessly at the ball Milo controls until one of them, shoving hard against him, kicks the ball at an angle across the field, away from all three of them, away even from either goal. The ball hits my flute case, which I have swung awkwardly in front of me to protect myself. The flute case whams my nose and drops to the ground. I bend over, my hands up against my stinging face, and moan helplessly.

Trilby dances around me, her thin red hair blowing threadlike across her eyes. "Hannah, your nose—it's bleeding. Oh, geez." Then, clutching her violin, she shouts, "Does somebody have some toilet paper?"

Toilet paper?

Gordy Fishbeck says he thinks there's some trailing from Neal Garrett's butt and everybody laughs.

I turn and head blindly back to the auditorium. "Wait—here." Milo is beside me and hands me a white, pressed cotton handkerchief, which he's pulled out of his pocket. This is more surprising than the call for toilet paper.

"Thanks," I say, and bury my nose in it.

"Here's another one . . ." Roman hands me an identical handkerchief. I am stunned. Handkerchiefs are like artifacts in a museum.

Milo seems to read my thoughts and smiles at me—a broad smile that momentarily makes me forget my misery. "Our mother makes us carry them."

"They're the sign of a gentleman." Roman grimaces. I don't think he smiles much.

"This is the first time they've been of any use," Milo says. His face is even more beautiful close-up than at a distance in the hallway or onstage at an assembly.

"Please thank her for me," I say. The throbbing is settling down a little.

"She'll be thrilled," Milo says. His eyes are concentrating on my face.

Mimi Manderino asks if I've broken my nose.

"I don't think so," I say.

Trilby says she'll call her mom to come and get us, but Mimi says no, we don't have to do that, because Milo can take us home in his car. She says this like she's his wife, and I remember that Milo and Mimi are going together and feel disappointed and then dumb for feeling any attraction to him at all. Such a hopeless attraction.

"No. I'm okay, really—" I say.

"I think it's a good idea," Trilby says. "I'm afraid you'll faint on the way home." More likely *she'll* faint. She pales at the sight of my blood.

"Come on," Milo says. "I'm parked over there." He points at the street on the south side of the field.

The rest of the guys have already gone back to playing as Milo leads me, Trilby, Mimi and Roman, who has retrieved my flute, off the field toward his car.

Next to the car, I wait for Milo to unlock the back door. "No, you sit in the front, Hannah," he says. "Don't want you to get dizzy."

Mimi is standing by the front door on the passenger side, and her face changes, like a small strangulation is taking place behind her skin. She looks through the glass at Milo, but then she turns to me. "Sure," she says, changing places with me.

Milo's 4Runner smells new. Enjoy this ride, I think. It'll be the last in this car. We drop Trilby off first, because she lives a block closer to school than I do. When we're parked in front of my house, I say this really dumb thing. I say, "I'll clean the handkerchiefs and get them back to you."

Mimi lets out this snort: "I'm sure they want them back." She laughs.

"With a little salt . . ." I sound like "Hints from Heloise."

Milo leans forward, his arm on the back of my seat.

"That'd be nice," he says. "I'll come pick 'em up tomorrow night." He wipes a smudge of blood off my cheek and smiles. He makes my stomach curl, but it stops when he glances back at Mimi. I realize he has said it for her. They are having some kind of fight.

"Thanks again," I say, opening the door. "Thanks, Roman," I call back to him.

He nods.

"Tomorrow night," Milo says before I close the door. He looks back at Mimi, whose jaw is set.

"It's okay," I say. "I'll bring them to school tomorrow."

I think Roman smiles for the first time.

Mimi gets in the front seat and they take off. They are not a happy couple, I think.

The next day Milo comes over to the lunch table where I eat with Trilby and Hilary Watson and tells me my nose looks none the worse for wear. "You've still got my hankie, though." He is teasing me.

His face, so close to mine, makes me nervous. "Oh, I forgot. I—I . . ." Stammer. Stammer.

He grins. He likes making me nervous, I think. "I'll come over tonight after seven, okay?"

I nod my head. "Okay."

"See you then."

"See you." A burning under my skin rises up my neck. I look at Trilby and Hilary and snicker behind my hands. Hilary's eyes are big as baseballs. "Oooh-whee, Momma! I can't believe what I just saw."

Trilby shakes her head. "If he were coming to *my*

house tonight, I'd have to go have all my freckles lasered off for the occasion."

The three of us shriek behind cupped hands, finally relieving the nervous tension by throwing bits of sandwiches at each other.

Milo does come, although he doesn't arrive until eight-thirty, and I've tried a half dozen different hairstyles: hair coiled up at the sides, at the back, in a long pigtail, all of it hanging down, then behind the ear. I'm just about ready to cut bangs when the doorbell rings.

Mama, in the "solarium," looks startled: "Who could that be at this time of night?" As if it's three in the morning. Her theory is that only serial killers call after sundown. Milo looks preppy in a fresh blue oxford-cloth shirt with the sleeves rolled up. "Hey, Ziebarth." He smiles.

"Come in," I say, and introduce him to Mama.

I can see by her face that she is impressed by Milo's good looks, his height, his neat appearance, his polite manner. "Don't you have a coat?" she asks.

"Left it in the car," he says. "It's not that cold out, really."

"I never go out, you know," Mama says. "But I do know it's February."

My throat constricts. No, he doesn't know she doesn't go out. "Milo and his brother loaned me their hankies when I got a bloody nose yesterday," I say quickly. I am smiling way too much.

"Oh, *this* is the boy. She got the blood out with salt," she confides to Milo, who thankfully does not smirk.

Then in a stage whisper to me: "I can see why you spent so long ironing them."

"They're in here; I'll get them." I walk through the dining room and, then, standing in the middle of my bedroom, take a few calming breaths. The hankies are on the bureau. I look them over carefully. Are they too pressed? I shake them out and refold them. Are they pressed enough? I force myself back to Milo and Mama.

Mama is showing Milo the bonsai. "See how this needs clipping?" Their faces are bent over a crab-apple tree.

"Here they are," I say, handing Milo the hankies.

He holds them briefly. "Nice ironing," he says, a playful smirk on his lips. He pockets the hankies.

"Now, look, this one's already been clipped. You can see the difference." Mama's still holding class.

Milo bends to look. "What about this?" He points to a barky scraggle under some foliage. "Shouldn't that be clipped?"

Mama peers closer. "You're right. I missed it" She's pleased at his attention. "Well, aren't you the smarty-party!" She gives him a playful punch. She's wearing Daddy's old argyle socks with a plaid skirt, and it seems to me that she looks like a character in one of those bizarre movies where none of the characters resembles anyone in real life.

"I guess no one plays the piano." Milo grins at the barely visible Steinway.

Mama and I speak at the same time: "Hannah's daddy did," she says. "Daddy did," I say.

"He's passed on," Mama says.

"Dead," I say.

"Oh, I didn't know."

"It's okay," I say.

"Is the guitar his too?" He nods at the guitar case tucked in the corner next to the piano. "Can I see it?" Even while Mama is saying "Of course," he's already leaning across some plants to lift the guitar out of its spot.

We follow him into the living room, where he opens the case and lifts out the guitar. "It's a Martin! This is a great guitar." He sits at the edge of the sofa, the guitar on his knee, strumming and tuning, and then leans over to pull a pick out of its little box. "Here," he says, smiling at Mama, "this is the one song that everyone in your generation sings when they get hold of a guitar." He plays "Michael, Row the Boat Ashore."

It is the first time Mama and I have seen or heard this guitar since Daddy died. Milo plays notes, not just chords. When he lowers his head, I see Daddy—the same dark hair, the same pose—Daddy sitting on the edge of the sofa playing the guitar. Daddy. I feel my chin tremble and bite hard on my bottom lip. Mama's fingers are pressed against her lips, but it's the guitar she's looking at, not Milo.

Milo looks up at us and starts to sing, his voice a mellow baritone. When he gets to an interval, he says, "Sing with me."

Mama, who used to sing a lot, joins in singing harmony, tentatively at first, but her voice grows stronger, a light, clear soprano. I do not trust my voice and have to wait a verse before I join in. By the third verse, we are all in full voice, and we sound good, really good. Mama smiles as she sings.

"Hey!" Milo cries when we're done. "You guys sound great!"

Mama giggles like a girl.

I say, "You're pretty good yourself."

"I come from a musical family," he says. He starts up another song.

I realize that I come from a musical family too. Piano, flute, voice. Why did we stop making music?

After two more songs, Mama jumps up and asks, "Can you sight-read?" She's already digging through a basket of music behind the overstuffed chair. "Because Brian wrote a lullaby for Hannah when she was a baby—here it is!" She hands him a yellowed sheet of paper with musical notation written in Daddy's hand. He's printed the words of the "Seal Lullaby" neatly below each measure. The faded pink ring from a glass of Kool-Aid I set down on it years ago still stains the bottom of the sheet.

"Let me just play with it a minute," Milo says, laying the music on the coffee table. He's a quick study, picking out the melody line and soon adding chords.

Mama hums along softly. I watch Milo work in profile.

"Okay, I'm ready," he says. "I'm going to play an introduction." He begins, and when it's time to sing, we join in, but our singing is feeble: the remembrance of Daddy too strong. I have to stop to keep my chin from trembling, and Mama is reduced to a simple humming again. Milo, aware of our distress, sings out more strongly. He sings it as if he's known the lullaby as long as we have. He sings it like Daddy used to sing it. Through my blurred vision, he even looks like Daddy. It's then, when Milo sings the "Seal Lullaby," that I fall in love with him.

Sometimes I have violent feelings toward Mama. Like a few minutes ago at dinner. I have been practicing making rice dishes for more than a week, ever since Mrs. Fabiano told me that Milo loves rice. Mama notices this as we eat *risotto alla milanese* with a roast chicken I bought already cooked at the Thriftway. "Aren't we eating a lot of rice?" she asks, her head bent over the plate, sniffing.

"Move your head," I say. "I'm going to sprinkle Parmesan cheese over the top." I sprinkle it on with my fingers. "I grated this myself."

"Don't use your fingers that way, Hannah. Use a spoon." She tastes the rice. "What's in it?" she asks. She drinks water.

"Saffron and fennel—it's Italian. I got the recipe out of the paper. 'Entice with Rice!' Do you like it?"

"You're like your daddy. He always liked to try out all those different kinds of recipes with the funny names—jambalaya. You remember when he made jambalaya?"

"Yes, but this is Italian." I eat a mouthful and wonder if Mrs. Fabiano has made *risotto alla milanese* for her family. Are the Fabianos from Milan? I can't remember. I am pleased with the taste of the rice.

Mama picks at her chicken now and pushes the rice onto the lip of the plate. "I miss potatoes," she says.

The violent feeling rushes in on me. I want to belt her one. Realizing this makes me weak with guilt. Mama is so alone and so helpless without Daddy. The idea that I, her only child, her daughter, would have such feelings makes me ill, and I clutch my throat with the hand that isn't clenched into a fist. I struggle to speak: "I can bake you a potato in the microwave. It only takes six minutes."

"Oh, no, I can eat a little more rice this one time." She places a hand on the fist in my lap. "You take such good care of me, Hannah, and I am grateful. I don't want to be any trouble to you." But she doesn't eat any more rice.

Nor does she ask me why I've been practicing rice dishes. Like an idiot, maybe because I need to talk to someone—anyone—even someone who doesn't really want to hear it—I decide to tell her. "Rice is Milo's favorite food. His mother told me it's practically the only thing he'll eat." I force a shrill little laugh. "Besides Ho Hos."

She pushes the plate away from her. "You're practicing rice dishes for Milo? Why?" The color rises on her neck.

"We're having a baby, Mama—"

"What has that got to do with it?"

"When I tell him about the baby, he's going to want to marry me—it's only natural."

36

"You're fifteen! You can't get married."

"I'm having a baby. A baby needs parents." I need parents, I think. Two of them.

"What makes you think he'll want to marry you?"

"Milo's decent, he'll—"

"And we don't have enough room . . ."

I stare at her. I hadn't even thought of Milo and me and the baby living with her. "I know that," I say. "But Milo's family has plenty of room. They even have an apartment over the garage that nobody's using." I know this, because Milo took me up there the day we made up after he nearly drowned me. We lay on the bed under the sloping eaves. We are like married people already—Milo and me.

"Hannah, listen to me." Mama turns in her chair and our knees are touching. She pats my legs lightly as she talks. "If Daddy were here, he would not let you marry. He would say you are far too young. You have to finish your schooling, college . . ."

If Daddy were here, maybe I wouldn't be pregnant. I say, "Tell that to the baby," and shove my chair back from her touch.

"There are lots of nice couples who can't have babies . . ." Her hands cup into a ball, which she seems to be smoothing as if she too were making a baby. "People who are just yearning to adopt—"

"No." I stand up. "No. It's *my* baby." I leave the room to be away from her, but she follows me past the precious bonsai to the front door, which I open.

"Don't go," Mama says, but I'm already out the door. "Please, Hannah." Even without looking I know she is standing behind the screen door, her fingers covering her mouth, her elbows squeezed against her torso. It is her anxious pose. "I can't allow you to go," she calls.

I turn at the bottom of the steps. "Stop me, Mama. Come and stop me." Our eyes meet across the expanse of the porch. Her shoulders slump and tremble. She steps back from the screen. "Please, Hannah." One hand makes a weak gesture toward me.

"Stop me." If she would only step onto the porch, I would stay. If she would only open the screen door, I would stay. If she would only turn the knob.

She shakes her head and steps back. The sun is bright in the west and reflects on the screen, so that I barely see her shadow behind it, but I know I have made her cry again. I run down the slope of the lawn, down McClelland Street and onto 8th South. I don't stop running until I've crossed 10th East and am out of breath. It is then that I see Bishop Kelsey out on his lawn. We're Mormons, and he's the bishop of our ward, our congregation. He's just turned the sprinklers on. I've been to church only a couple of times since Daddy died, and I want to cross the street and avoid him, but he's already seen me. I force a smile. He's standing on the sidewalk by the time I reach his house, which is third from the corner.

"Hi, Hannah, how are ya?" He shakes my hand like he does in church. "How's your mother?"

"We're both fine," I say. It's what people expect me to say. It's what he expects. No one seems to think it odd that Mama never leaves the house. He nods.

"Really?" His eyes bore into me. Can he tell I'm pregnant? Do I have that pregnant "glow" I've read about?

"Sure," I say. "She likes taking care of her bonsai plants and—things." I can't think of anything else that Mama likes to do except fret.

He nods. He knows about the bonsai, because he visits her every few months as do other people in our ward. It makes them feel good to look after her. "And you—what are you up to these days?"

Fornication. It's the only word I can think of. It makes me laugh a silly laugh, and I say, "Nothing much. Just enjoying the vacation, I guess."

"Still playing the flute?"

"Once in a while." I can't remember the last time I opened my flute case outside of school orchestra rehearsals.

"Well, it's a real talent. I'd like to have you play in church again." He smiles. He's a pretty nice guy, really, but I want to get out of there. "How about it?"

"I'd have to work something up," I say. "I'm pretty rusty."

"Do it, and I'll call you in a couple of weeks." He's got his hands in the pockets of his jeans and I wonder if he's trying to look casual to make me comfortable. Adults do hokey things like that.

"I'll do it for sure," I say. "Gotta go." I sort of dance away from him down the hill.

"Nice to see you, Hannah," he calls to me. He really is pretty nice.

"Yeah, same here." I walk on down the hill. He probably wouldn't like me if he knew I was pregnant.

Probably wouldn't invite me to church even to play the flute. Probably would excommunicate me. I run faster. I'm enjoying my paranoia. And it is paranoia. Bishop Kelsey—Bill—was Daddy's good friend. They belonged to a group who played basketball together on Thursday nights.

Daddy. At 9th East I stop for the light to change and after crossing the street turn right. It was Daddy who taught me to cook rice: bring the water, salt, and butter to a boil, add the rice, cover, and simmer exactly twenty minutes. It's so simple you wonder why anyone ever buys that sickening Minute rice junk. Daddy also taught me how to make rice pudding with the leftover white rice. We used whipping cream instead of milk, and eggs, vanilla, raisins, cinnamon, and nutmeg. I could eat it all week long. Daddy and I cooked together since I was three. Together it was fun. Alone, it's just another chore. You shouldn't have burped, Daddy. I try never to burp.

Down the street past 7th South there is a commotion. People standing about with signs. It isn't until I cross the street and am in front of the Dodo Restaurant that I can read the signs: "Stop Abortion Now." One man and three women are holding signs. And on the strip of lawn next to the sidewalk, an easel is set up with a large poster and pictures on it. They yell at the cars coming out of the parking lot. It must be closing time. When I get closer I see that the plain brick building is the Planned Parenthood office. I have never noticed it until this minute. I feel like I'm dreaming and that the building has just grown up in front of me, because I'm pregnant, because I didn't plan my parenthood. It all seems calculated.

An old Chevrolet drives slowly down the narrow driveway out to 9th East. "Murderer!" the four people shout. One woman is especially passionate. She shrieks it several times and strikes her fist on the trunk of the car as it passes.

I am stopped on the sidewalk. I don't want to pass by them in case they shout at me. I am guilty of so much. There are references to scriptures on each sign. I try to memorize them so I can look them up when I get home. Numbers 35:30. Jeremiah 1:5. Psalms 82: 3&4. Isaiah 44:2. When I turn my head for a second, I can't remember any of them. And when I turn back, the man is throwing the signs into the back of an old Ford truck parked in front of the building. The parking lot is empty, and they are leaving. I continue slowly down the sidewalk and stop in front of the poster, which shows an aborted fetus pulled to pieces. A tiny hand is in the right-hand corner. A foot. A head and torso. I shrink back. The woman who yelled "Murderer" comes up behind the poster to remove it. When she sees my face, a tight smile forms on her lips. "God hates murderers," she says, her low voice gravelly from yelling. I hate the pictures of the mutilated fetuses. I feel like I've been subjected to an obscenity. I move away from her and then turn back. "I don't think God thinks much of you either," I say. I hate her even more than the pictures.

I want to run down the sidewalk. Fast. I manage to

walk. I look back to see if the truck will come after me, but they move slowly down the street in the opposite direction, two of the women sitting in the back. I run until I come to a lot with a half-finished apartment complex on it. There are wood planks stacked close to the sidewalk, and I sit down on them and look out at the traffic along 9th East. I am crying, but I don't care. I can't carry this secret—this pregnancy—around by myself anymore. I think of the Planned Parenthood sign on the building. If I didn't plan before the pregnancy, I can plan now, but first I need to tell Milo. Then the two of us can plan together. I make a promise to myself. I will tell him before the 4th of July, which is a week away. It will be such a relief to share this. I sing the "Seal Lullaby" to myself: "Oh, hush thee, my baby, the night is behind us . . ." It calms me.

My baby is a boy. I know this, not from any test, but from my gut. He looks like this baby I saw in a Michelin commercial, floating in a tire. Dark, wispy hair and dark eyes smiling, his little fat hand grasping at something off camera. He looks like Milo. Those baby ads are a real meltdown. I can't even get through a diaper commercial without wiping my eyes. I'm going to use the diaper with the blue trim and padding up front where boys need it most.

When I walk in the front door, Mama is bent over a Chinese juniper that I brought from outside that morning. She murmurs to her "babies" but stops when I close the door. She turns and looks at me. She doesn't look scared anymore. She's no longer afraid of my leaving her forever. She has thought of something. "Hannah," she says. "If you're so sure that Milo will marry you, why haven't you told him yet?"

Mama, 1. Hannah, 0.

Not surprisingly, Bishop Kelsey shows up at the house a few days after I met him on the sidewalk. Some might say he's inspired, that he can see that I'm in trouble and has come by to help. I think it's just my bum luck. I don't want to talk to him right now. And for a while I think I won't have to. I can hear his and Mama's voices out in the living room. Perhaps he has come to see just her, but Mama calls me out of my bedroom, where I am hanging freshly stolen roses upside down from the ceiling in little bunches tied with twine. I press the twine into the ceiling with a thumbtack. My ceiling is riddled with thumbtack holes. I keep the roses in water for a day or so because I like them when they're full and sensuous looking and smell good. Roses are simply the wisest thing in the universe.

"Hi, Hannah!" Bishop Kelsey stands when I walk into the room like I'm some old person or something. Mama's sitting in the overstuffed chair by the fireplace and her head is down so I can't see her eyes. This is how I know that she has told him of my "condition." That's what Mama calls the pregnancy: a condition, like I've just developed scales or something.

"How're you doing?" I sit near the TV cabinet to avoid having to shake his hand.

"Great, great." He nods his head a lot. He's the same

age as my daddy. They were friends. How come he didn't die of a burp? He glances at my stomach. Then he sits on the sofa with one leg slung over the other and plays with a little braided piece of leather on his loafer. He's wearing a jacket and tie: his bishop's uniform.

"Hannah." Mama raises her head. "I've told Bishop Kelsey about—"

Your condition.

"—your condition." She smiles at me like I'm a stranger.

"Oh?" I want to say she shouldn't have, but I'm not in a rude mood.

"If you don't want to talk about it with me . . ." Bishop Kelsey is blushing. I like him better.

"And he agrees with me"—Mama cuts him off—"that it would be best for you and the baby if you gave it up for adoption."

"Well, that isn't exactly what I said," Bishop Kelsey says. "I said it was an option."

"I'm getting married," I say. "I don't want to give the baby away."

"And—" Bishop Kelsey begins.

"You just can't," Mama says. "I can't take care of you and a baby."

"I don't need you to take care of me," I say.

"Marriage is also an option," Bishop Kelsey manages to fit in.

"Tell her she's too young," Mama demands of Bishop Kelsey.

"I think Hannah knows how young she is," he says.

He smiles at me. He is not exactly cooperating with Mama, and I smile back.

"Well, lots of teenage girls miscarry, maybe she will too." She talks like I'm not in the room.

"Or I could have an abortion," I say. "I was down at the Planned Parenthood . . ." I don't say that I just happened by it.

"Hannah, it's a sin. How can you talk like that? It's an unforgivable sin."

"And it's not a sin to wish a miscarriage on me?"

Mama's neck blotches slightly. "I didn't say that."

Bishop Kelsey says that this is a difficult time for both Mama and me and that the important thing is that our relationship as mother and daughter stay intact. I think he is embarrassed to be in the same room with us. I know I'm pretty embarrassed myself. And what is so special about this mother-daughter relationship that I should be concerned about it? I'm in a rude mood now and can't think of an answer.

Mama stares at the carpet. "It's just that I'm so worried," she says.

Tell me something new.

Even though I'm only fifteen, I have a job at the Burger Bar downtown on Main Street. Mama's cousin, Sewell Satterfield, owns the place, and though I'm not absolutely sure, I think Mama more or less begged him to take me on. She's pretty good at playing the widow-down-to-the-last-mite role. Anyway, he was happy to have me at an hourly wage that exceeds baby-sitting pay by a nickel. But as Mama says, "Every little bit helps. Beggars can't be choosy." So *that's* what we've become: beggars.

I can't work the cash register, because I'm not sixteen, and I can't use the meat slicer—you have to be eighteen to do that. I can make fries, dipping the wire basket in and out of the spitting lard. Burger Bar hasn't heard about polyunsaturates yet. I'm always surprised to see a repeat customer. When the grease makes me sick to my stomach, Bliss, the manager, lets me cut tomatoes and onions for a while, or I carry around a spray bottle of cleaner and wipe off tables and countertops.

I want to tell Milo about our baby at my house in the afternoon, sitting on the porch swing together. Milo liked that swing from the first moment he saw it. That was before the Marimekko pillows I made were stolen. I picture us there, me with my head on his shoulder, my hand patting his chest where his pocket is. I will start cautiously, asking him if he likes kids. And he will say, "Sure. I come from a huge family. What's there not to like about Rose and Gina? They're a kick." He will cover my hand with his and continue, "Roman's a throwaway, though." He will not mean it. I will laugh and dig my head a little deeper into his neck, and I will tell him. I will call him by name. "Milo," I'll say. "I'm pregnant. I've checked with a doctor, and I'm pregnant. You and I are going to have a baby."

He'll be shocked, and then he'll be concerned the way he was when my nose bled from the soccer ball hit.

He'll want to know how long I've known, and I'll tell him. "Almost three months."

He'll be hurt that I've kept it to myself for so long. Then he'll get Daddy's guitar and sing me the "Seal Lullaby." I'll tell him how I've been singing to our baby from the first moment I suspected I was pregnant. "He'll know the words when he's born," I'll say. Milo will laugh at me, but I'll tell him, "Really. Fetuses can hear their mothers singing to them. It can hear you now, so be good."

And he'll lean his head down, lift my shirt, and kiss my belly right on the skin and say, "Can we keep it? Please, can we keep it?" I've known Milo in some tender moments, and I'm pretty sure what his reaction will be.

But when I finally do call him to say I have something to talk about with him and invite him to the house and say I'll make lemonade, he says he can't come, because he and his dad are playing golf at the university. "I'll come and see you at work. Save your break for me."

"Oh, not at work. How about tomorrow morning at my house—"

"What is the big deal? Anyway, I have a dentist appointment in the morning. There's no way my mother will let me cancel it. I'll see you tonight. Save me some fries."

"Come alone," I say, but I don't know if he hears me.

Even though I'm driving now, I don't drive to work, because it costs too much to park. I take the bus. Besides, I figure Milo will hang around until my shift is finished and take me home. He'll want to talk about our future.

Five minutes before Milo arrives, this homeless guy, Old Faithful, appears. I saw him sleeping between two Dumpsters out in back one time. I don't know who gave him the name Old Faithful or even why, but that's what everyone calls him. Today he's wearing a plaid blazer with worn, dirty cuffs.

"You got a new coat," Bliss, the night manager, says. She stands back from the counter to avoid smelling him, but I can smell the stale odor of him way over at the fry machine. I blink a few times to keep from making a face. The new boy, Dennis, stands behind the cash register. "Can I help you?" His Adam's apple races up and down while his nose shrinks into his face. I want to laugh.

I doubt Old Faithful even notices. He holds out his filthy, creased hand with a few coins in it. "An order of fries, please." His voice is asthmatic and his watery eyes look over at me and the tray of fries I have just salted.

Dennis looks at the money. "Fries are seventy-five cents an order," he says, businesslike. And then as if Old Faithful might not know: "You've only got thirty-two cents." Dennis rubs his index finger under his nose, hoping to keep Old Faithful's rotting smell out of his nostrils.

Old Faithful stares into his open palm, his head trembling slightly. "Could I buy thirty-two cents' worth of fries?" You can hear the phlegm in his voice. "Please."

It is seven in the evening when most of the downtown workers have gone home. Only one woman near the front of the place sits eating a ham and cheese and one of Burger Bar's Salivating Shakes, which to me sounds like a shake made with spit.

Dennis turns to Bliss with raised eyebrows. Can he sell thirty-two cents' worth of fries? Two girls walk into the store, and, catching a whiff of Old Faithful, stand well back from him. Bliss shakes her head. No. The answer is no. I could turn around and start a new batch of fries, and avoid the old man's suffering gaze, but I don't.

"Sorry, sir." Dennis's voice is efficient. "We can't do that." He looks over the old man's shoulders and addresses the two girls. "Welcome to Burger Bar. Can I help you?"

"Two Bravo Burgers, two orders of fries, and two Cokes." The girls sidestep Old Faithful as he turns toward the door. He picks three uneaten fries off one of the tables that hasn't been bussed yet, and thrusts them into his mouth. Then he takes the wrapper and licks the ketchup and mayonnaise half-dried to the inside of the paper.

The girls see it too and grimace. "Geez," one of them whispers. "Gross. They shouldn't let people like him in here."

I feel sick and know the baby didn't cause it. I check my pocketbook under the counter to see if I have any money, and it is the weirdest thing—I have only thirty-two cents just like Old Faithful. Even if I give it to him, he still won't have enough for an order of fries. I feel pathetic.

Then Bliss's hand is on my arm. "We're not a home-

49

less shelter or a soup kitchen. The customers would resent it if we gave food away to some people and made others pay full price. Do you understand?"

I nod, although I don't agree, and slip the coins back into my wallet. The truth is we have to throw away burgers and fries that have been sitting longer than a half hour. Perfectly good food and we throw it out. I hope Old Faithful knows. He can wait at the Dumpsters.

It doesn't take looking out the window to know that Milo has arrived. The bass of his Blaupunkt stereo hurls Megadeth at us. The front windows tremble.

"What the . . ." Bliss looks across the store and out the window. The Toyota 4Runner is double-parked directly in front of the restaurant. Gordy Fishbeck and Mimi Manderino climb out with Milo. Milo locks the car with the motor running and Megadeth booming into the street: "Mama! Mama!"

My breathing tightens, and I have to think about relaxing. Am I wheezing? Am I making a noise? I thought he would come alone. Didn't I say that it was important, that I have to see him alone? Or did I forget to say that? Have I just assumed that if it were important, he would automatically think to come alone? I should have said, "Don't bring an entourage." I should have said that.

Mimi walks in first wearing these cute shorts and a halter. I saw them at the Gap but couldn't afford them. I feel stifled inside my yellow and brown polyester Burger Bar suit. I know the hat looks ridiculous on me. I can't wear hats. Still I manage a pretty cheerful "Hi" when they amble up to the yellow Formica counter.

Dennis stands next to me and says, "Welcome to Burger Bar! Can I help you?" He pushes his mammoth glasses back up on his nose. He is so stiff, so genetically dweebed.

Milo's dimples always appear when he suppresses a laugh. "What have you got to give me that I don't already have?"

"How about an Adam's apple?" This is Fishbeck.

"I like your outfit," Mimi teases Dennis. I take her teasing personally. I'm wearing an identical outfit and know it is hateful. No one has to say it. Why is she here?

"What do you want with your lard?" I ask. It is better to take the offensive with this group, although it's hard when your throat is closed off.

Milo smiles. "Can we just have lard, plain?"

"Yeah, but it costs extra."

"Fries and Cokes, then." He turns to Fishbeck and Mimi. "Save me a seat," he says, and waves them off with his arm. They move together like cows toward a table.

Dennis goes to fill their order. I lean forward across the counter and whisper: "I thought you were coming alone. I want to talk to you *alone*."

"I *was* coming alone and then Fishbeck and Manderino showed up." He shrugs. "What could I do?"

"Why have you left the car running?" I don't want to ask this. I sound irritable, but the bass of his car seems to bounce the whole block. It seems to me he wants to make a quick getaway. I almost say this but swallow it down. "You could get a ticket," I say instead.

He exaggerates a shudder. "Oh, no, not a ticket! What will I do?" He pretends to bite his nails.

"You're such a brat," I say.

He leans over the bar. "You like brat."

"Guess so." I can smile a little now.

"Know so," he says, and smacks his lips.

Dennis has the order ready on a tray and rings it up. Milo pulls a twenty-dollar bill out of his pocket. I can't help thinking that twenty bucks is almost five hours of work for me. Milo has never worked for money that I know of. Our child won't have to either. He picks up the tray and nods at me. "Come and sit with us."

I look back at Bliss, who is packing a couple of burgers into Styrofoam boxes. She's scowling. My friends annoy her. I look at my watch. "I go on break in five minutes," I tell Milo. "I want to talk to you alone. Meet me out in back, okay?" I look back again at Bliss to see if she hates me personally, but her head is turned. I'm relieved when Milo leaves the counter, and I busy myself making more fries.

What will Milo do? I wonder. Will he drive Mimi and Fishbeck home and come back for me so we can talk more?

Laughter breaks out at Milo's table, and Milo whistles between his fingers. They watch a cop walking around the 4Runner, looking down the street, scratching his head.

Fishbeck pretends to speak as the cop: "Duh, what's this doing here? Duh."

Mimi covers a snicker with her hand.

Milo jumps up and runs out the door. "Oh, Officer," he calls. When the door shuts we can't hear him any longer. But I can tell that he is telling the cop a story; his hands dance in gesture, a smile plays on his lips. There's nothing as charming as Milo telling a story, I think.

Then he and the cop shake hands, and Milo gets into the 4Runner and moves it down the street.

Mimi turns to me. "Can you believe it?" she says. "Is he smooth or what?"

I nod at her. He is smooth to his butt. I know. Smooth. Smooth. Smooth.

"He's so lucky." Fishbeck slurps through the ice for more Coke. "I would have been handcuffed and arrested by now."

When Milo struts back into the restaurant, they applaud him. Even the two girls who don't know him applaud. He bows modestly with his head, grins, and looking at me, says, "I told you not to worry."

I smile back, feeling relaxed for the first time. I will have to get used to having Milo take care of things, I think. It will be such a relief.

In a few minutes he comes to the counter and says, "Mimi's got to get back, so let's go out in back and you can tell me your B-B-BIG secret." He lets through the door cut into the counter, which is a big no-no. Bliss reminds us constantly not to allow customers on the working side of the counter. It's practically her mantra.

"Has this big secret anything to do with me?" Milo asks.

"Of course." My voice is strangely cheerful. When we step out into the alley, Bliss is seated on a box next to the door, smoking. She looks at her watch and nods at us.

"Let's walk down to the end of the alley," I say. We pass the back of the Tall Man's Shop, which is now closed, then Wong's House, a Chinese food place. Two young Chinese guys are also smoking, quietly speaking in Chinese to each other. They watch us briefly. We pass the back of the bookstore and the electronics store and then we are at the end of the alley, a brick wall, which is the back of a bank. To the left is a parking lot. Against the brick wall are lined five Dumpsters, one for each business whose back faces the alley. Each has a painted name on it identifying the owner: Burger Bar, Wong's House, and so on all the way to Banc One.

We stop in front of the Dumpsters, which are overflowing with bulging plastic bags. "Whew," Milo says, taking one step back. "Geez, how can you stand working here?"

"I don't work out here," I say.

He circles his arms loosely around my waist. "You smell good, though." He's smiling. Relieved, I lean into him with my hips and push my knees between his legs. I want him to forget the alley. I want to forget it myself. We kiss a long time. "Hey, hey, Ziebarth," he mutters into my cheek. The two Chinese men are watching us. I don't really care. Bliss has disappeared.

We kiss again. I want to suck his face off. I don't care about moderation and public space. I don't care where I am.

"Ziebarth, baby . . . ," Milo whispers, and I am jolted into remembering the baby—I push him away gently. "Wait . . ." And covering his mouth with my hand when he tries to kiss me again, I say, "I have to tell you . . ."

He backs away a little and I can see from the way his lips have tightened that he's annoyed. This isn't the way I want to tell him. Not this way in front of reeking Dumpsters and two Chinese guys laughing at us halfway down the alley. Then I think of Mama and Bishop Kelsey talking as if I'm not there, as if the decision about what happens with the baby is theirs to make, not mine.

"I'm going to have a baby," I blurt out. "I'm pregnant. It's for sure. I went to a doctor."

Milo squints as if not comprehending. "What do you mean?"

"I—that is, *we*—are going to have a baby."

Milo's mouth closes, his chin juts forward, and then his arm comes up and he shoves me hard against the shoulder so that I fall back against a Dumpster. It hurts everywhere and I crumple into myself. "*We* are not having a baby. *You're* having a baby. Not *we*. I used protection." His voice is low but emphatic.

"Not the first time"—I struggle to whisper—"the night of the Lakers game."

Milo's hand is around my throat, pinning me to the

55

Dumpster. "Every time, Hannah, every single time. I'm not taking the blame for your mistake."

It is the first time he has called me by my first name. He's always called me Ziebarth before, even when we were making love.

"I'm pregnant, and it's your child. I haven't slept with anyone but you. It's yours," I say.

Briefly his hand leaves my throat, only to return in a balled fist against my face. Everything is in slow motion. I see his fist coming but can do nothing. No one has ever slugged me before. My head rattles on my neck before it smacks against the Dumpster. "Whore!" he says. He rubs the blood off his fist and walks away.

Milo wasn't the first boy to kiss me but he was the first one to bite me. I said "Ouch," and he said, "Let me lick it better." When the camisole came off, I kissed him fiercely. Too fiercely. He said, "Slow down. It's better slow." How did he know?

It was wonderful that first time with Milo. He was tender and practiced. Only now do I realize he was practiced, very practiced. What do you call a boy who's a slut?

Only now, sitting here in the gravelly alley, against a Dumpster, holding the side of my face, which seems to be bleeding, do I have a clue about sadness.

Bliss drives me home after she bandages the cut near my eye. I can feel it swelling, can feel my eye closing. Bliss says I should see a doctor and then the police. "You should have the SOB arrested for assault," she says.

"He didn't mean to," I say.

"Bull," she says.

I stand on the sidewalk in front of my house and watch Bliss speed away. It's late enough that the sunlight has faded to dark gold, and the sunglasses I wear to hide my discolored eye seem ridiculous. Still, I keep them on, because Rosa Benson is sitting on her front porch watching me. I think of a vocabulary word I learned in English last year: *nemesis:* retribution and punishment. Rosa Benson is my nemesis. I open the garage door and get in the Prizm. I think if I can see Milo's face I will know for sure that he didn't mean to hit me. I'll prove Bliss wrong.

The streetlights in Milo's neighborhood are made to look like gas lamps from the last century and so are the houses, which copy an English or French country look. At least that's what I imagine such houses to look like. I've never been anywhere except down south to see Bryce and Zion canyons, and I can hardly remember them. I was about eight, and we stopped in Annabella on the way home to see Grandma Satterfield, who didn't seem at all crazy to me, and when we got home, Uncle Sewell called to say that Grandma had died while taking a nap after dinner. After eating her favorite butterscotch pudding topped with whipped cream. Now I consider butterscotch flavoring a danger and never eat it. I don't drink pop either. It makes you burp.

I am walking up Milo's street in the dark except for the glow of those precious streetlamps. The Prizm is parked in the next block. When I reach his house, I step onto the lawn at the side of the driveway where the shadows of a giant sycamore tree camouflage me. The 4Runner is parked under the portico, where I know Mr. Fabiano does not like it parked, because it blocks the front door. He wants all the cars in the garages at the side of the house.

The windows are all lit up, even Milo's room, but from where I'm standing, I can't see anyone in the house. I move out of the shadow of the tree until I'm at the side of the house, looking into the dining room window. From there, I can also see the hall and the living room. No one.

Then I hear them. All of them. They're in the back by the pool. I hear Milo playing the guitar. Slowly, I make my way along the side of the house and crouch under the lilac bush out of reach of the floodlight at the corner of the house directly under the roof. Gina, Rose, and Tony are in the pool. The twins' water wings remind me of the afternoon a few weeks ago when I played in the pool with them. The afternoon when Gina wanted me to come and live with them. Tony lies on his stomach on a bright green vinyl raft, using his arms as paddles to escape the twins, who want to knock him off. The girls screech when they are almost successful. Mrs. Fabiano, in a cool, modulated voice, reminds them that it is night and they need to be considerate of the neighbors. "Keep your voices down," she says. She barely lifts her head from the chaise lounge when she talks. Her dress is flowery and off the shoulders. I think I can smell her fragrance. Perhaps it is only the lilacs.

Mr. Fabiano, whose lips are pressed tight in mild irritation, plays chess with Roman at the round metal table, under a bright canvas umbrella. "Focus, Roman" he says. "You could have taken my knight right there." He makes a small gesture with his hand. "You need to concentrate, son."

Roman nods and grimaces.

The guitar music stops. "I get to play the winner." This is Milo's voice. He is sitting at the far side of the patio, too close to the house for me to see him.

I want to see his face, because then I will know for sure he didn't mean it. He didn't mean to hit me. Milo is just scared. I know about scared people and how they take swipes at you. Mama does it with her tongue. It's because she feels helpless and needs to bark at somebody and I'm the only one to bark at. I'm pretty sure I'm right about this. Milo went farther, but it's because he's a boy and athletic and real physical, and swinging is the first thing he does. It's intuitive, like a grizzly bear.

My foot is asleep and I try to change positions, try to stretch forward to glimpse Milo's face. Something in the bush cracks, and Roman and his father, who are sitting closest to me, both turn their heads and look straight at me. My heart begins to boogie in my chest and my throat swells, but I can't close my eyes. We stare through the lilac bush at each other. I wait, holding my breath for one of them to say, "What are you doing, Hannah? Why are you hiding in that bush?"

I can't think of an answer.

They turn back to their game. I've forgotten how to breathe, how to blink, how to move my limbs. Everything hurts.

Finally Mr. Fabiano triumphs. Roman's white chess pieces lie like corpses close to Mr. Fabiano's sherbet dish, while Mr. Fabiano's black pieces still stand tall on the checkered board. Now Milo will come to the table and play, I think. Now I will see his face and know.

But Milo is no longer interested when Mr. Fabiano calls him. "Later," he says. "I've got to get Mimi home."

Mimi? I have not heard or seen Mimi. Mimi is here? Then I hear her voice. "Thanks for the sorbet, Mrs. Fabiano."

Sorbet? Aren't we talking sherbet? I hate myself for not knowing the language of the rich. I hate myself for caring. *Thank you for the sorbet, Mrs. Fabiano.*

A little madness sets in right there, if I were forced to pinpoint moments of madness to a jury:

—*When were you first aware of your madness, Miss Ziebarth?*

—*That's easy. It was when Mimi said* sorbet *instead of* sherbet.

—*And how did this madness manifest itself?*

—*I thought I was a lilac tree . . .*

—*You thought you were . . .*

—*a lilac tree, but then I knew I was a girl, and I scampered—skulked actually—along the side of the Fabianos' house, around the corner, and opened the back of the 4Runner and got in behind the backseat and covered myself with that plaid blanket, that sometime mattress that Milo keeps back there. I hid under the blanket.*

—No doubt you were a little mad.

—No doubt.

I am thrilled by my own daring. My heart races. What if they catch me? What will I say?

Minutes later I hear the front door of the house open, hear Mimi's musical voice—The voice of St. Theresa herself—say, "No I can't go overnight. My parents won't let me."

"They won't let you go camping?"

"Of course they let me go camping." The passenger door opens. I hold my breath. "But they're not going to let me go camping alone with you and that's for sure." Mimi's voice is teasing.

"Well, tell them you're going with someone else, then. Tell them you're going with Ziebarth. They won't call her mother. She's loony." I swallow again and again. Big loud gulpy swallows. Swallows that fill the universe.

"Why don't you take Hannah camping?" Old Mimi's gone a-fishing.

Swallow. Swallow. Swallow. Still the lumps grow bigger.

"Hannah and I are through. I never should have broken it off with you." Milo's in the car now with the door closed. There is a rustling in the front seat. "Remember how much fun we used to have—"

"Don't!" Mimi says. Another rustle. Is he moving back behind the steering wheel? "I also remember how fast you took up with Hannah."

"She totally stalked me—"

I close my eyes against this lie. It makes me strangely calm. My cheek rests on the carpet floor. Under the blanket I am arranged in a fetal position. I want to suck my thumb, but I don't.

Milo's voice is low. "Hannah's a slut. I found that out today." His voice is filled with regret.

"Hannah?" Mimi sounds doubtful and hopeful at the same time. "How do you know that?"

"I just know. I don't want to tell you the rest, but she's pretty . . ." He pauses compassionately. "She's pretty skanky—if you know what I mean."

"I don't know . . ." Mimi falters. "I never thought of Hannah as—"

"Believe me, she's a slut. She knows moves I've never thought of before."

Under the blanket my face burns with misery. I shouldn't be here. It isn't helping. What was I thinking?

Milo turns on the ignition and revs the motor. A long pause. "Come here," he says. For a brief second I think he's found me and wants me to step over the backseat. There is a rustle of movement and I know he and Mimi are kissing. Mimi groans and sighs. Milo whispers things in her hair and face. Things I have heard a thousand times. I thought they were the first time he'd said them when he said them to me. So I'm learning a thing or two lying here in the back of his 4Runner. More rustling. He is working on her clothes now—on taking them off. She says, "No, not here. Your folks might see us." Pause pause pause. I am wretched with imagining.

Then a voice calls from outside the car. "Wait a minute." It's Roman. A major rustling goes on in the front. Roman comes from the side of the house. "Hold up," he says. "I left my putter in the back of your car and I want to practice for a while." He has one of those putting greens that automatically sends the ball back to you.

"Hurry up," Milo barks. He's impatient with hormonal interruptions.

I curl up as tight as I can when I hear the fifth door open. Roman moves the blanket that covers me. When he sees my face with the discolored eye that is now swollen completely shut, he gasps. Does he say "Hannah"?

I shake my head frantically at him, pleading not to give me away. He stands like a stunned gazelle waiting. His dead eye seems to drift to one side, looking for help.

"What's the matter?" Milo shouts from the front seat.

It takes Roman forever to speak. "Nothing," he says finally. And I realize that I'm not breathing at all. "I thought somebody had bent my iron." He reaches in to take it. I have to move my leg. He never takes his eyes off my face. He shuts the door and even through the window he stares at me. His right eye is the good eye. I know that now. You look into the right eye and you're looking at Roman and he's looking back.

"His iron is limp all the time." Milo snorts. He revs the engine and squeals out of the driveway onto the street toward Mimi's house, only a few blocks away.

He parks on the street in front of her house away from the streetlamp and stops the engine. "We're alone," he says.

Mimi laughs. "Except for a house full of my nearest and dearest."

"They're not likely to come out, are they?" Milo asks.

Nothing from Mimi.

They begin making out. Even from under the blanket I can hear the groping and groaning. I can hear spitting and sucking. I shove my fingers in my ears and pull the blanket tight around my head. But no amount of filling my ears can get me away from the movement of the car—a steady, familiar rhythm. My head hurts, but that's not why I'm crying silently, the water running down the side of my nose. I am thinking about my baby—my little girl—it must be a girl—a girl who will never have a father. I cry after the car stops shaking, after Mimi leaves to go into her house. I cry when Milo sings with the radio on the way home, when he parks the car in the garage and shuts the door. The radio keeps playing for a few minutes. It turns off automatically along with the lights. The last words I hear are from Beck: "I'm a loser, baby. So why don't ya kill me."

Mama has gone to bed when I get home, but she calls to me: "Where have you been?" Her voice quivers with anxiety.

"At the Fabianos'," I call from the bathroom. My face is a swollen mess. The cut below my closed eye looks like it might need stitches.

"You should have called," she says. "I was worried. I thought you'd be home after work."

"Sorry," I say. Sorry for living.

"Just a phone call to let me know—"

"Sorry. I'll remember next time."

"You know how worried I get."

"Yes," I say. When I touch the cut, a little blood comes out. I touch it with my finger and stripe my cheeks with it. More comes out and I dabble some on my chin. "War paint."

"What?" Mama calls from her bedroom.

"Nothing." I didn't know I'd spoken aloud. "Go to sleep. I'll talk to you in the morning. Okay?"

"I can't sleep when you're not here."

"I'm here now. Good night."

"I worry so."

"I know. Good night."

"I love you, you know."

"Good night." In the medicine cabinet, Daddy's old razor blades lie in a tiny box on the top shelf. I remove one. "This eye doesn't match this one—that's bad," I whisper to the bloody image. I run the corner of the blade alongside the good eye. The image groans. "Shhh . . ." I say. The blood runs darkly down the cheek. Now they match. Good, thick paint. I streak my face again across both cheeks and turn off the light.

My bedroom is lit with moonlight, so that when I pass the mirror above the chest of drawers I can see the stripes of blood I have painted on my face. "Savage," I whisper, and breathe my hot breath onto the mirror. The trees outside the window make shadowy imitations of themselves on the bedroom walls, and I pretend I'm in a primeval forest. Hannah, the beast of the jungle. I say "pretend," because I know that my bedroom is not really a jungle or a forest. I know that I'm not really a savage. It's an important distinction. I know I'm not crazy.

I know when I begin dancing quietly in a circle on the rug next to my bed that I'm pretending to do a ritual dance, but what kind of ritual? I have no idea. I let out a whoop accidentally. My moving arms made the whoop come out.

"Hannah?" Mama calls from her room just through the wall.

I stand like a grinning tree. I think I like being a tree.

"Hannah?"

Trees don't talk. Doesn't she know? I feel the sap move through me.

"Hannah, what was that noise?"

I shake my branches.

Then she is standing in the door frame squinting to see what I'm doing. She flicks on the light. "Oh, my lord." She is saying a little prayer, I guess. She says it again. "Oh, my lord, my lord." Vain repetitions. I wave my branches.

And Mama does what Mama does best—she shrinks into herself and looks like she might vomit. "Hannah, call 911. Your face is bleeding." Her hands are tiny fists covering her mouth. "Oh, Hannah, please call them."

You call 911, the tree thinks. If 911 would call Mama, then Mama could handle it. But Mama can't call 911. Mama works in one direction when it comes to the telephone. She never dials out. She never orders Chinese takeout or pizza. She never calls the carpet cleaners or the doctor. Once the doctor called her, though, and said, "Mrs. Ziebarth, Hannah, your fifteen-year-old daughter, is pregnant."

Mrs. Ziebarth whimpered and asked, "What will happen to me?"

I say to Mama, "Trees need to be outside. I need air." And I shove past her into the hall. "They need light," I say. And I turn on the lights in the dining room and the living room and in the "solarium," where several fellow trees, trees in miniature, are glad to see me. "I will save you," I say to them. And I pick three of them up, carrying them in my branches, and open the front door and throw them out onto the lawn.

Mama is behind me shouting, "No, Hannah! What are you doing?" I push past her and pick up the false cypress and the precious flowering quince and the dwarf birch, and I heave them onto the lawn as well.

Mama hovers near the door but not in the doorway, not on the porch. Even for the darlings, she cannot do that. She just cries, "Hannah, please."

"I am saving the trees," I call. And I throw the banyan fig down the slope of the lawn. The pot breaks, spilling the black soil and releasing the roots. "Free at last," I cry. I raise both arms high above my head and shake.

"Hannah, you need help!" Mama calls from the living room. She will not even stand in the open doorway.

"Then come and help me!" I call to her. "Come and get me. Or call 911. Help me, Mama."

She's crying out loud now. I run along the side of the house and grab several plants from the bleachers my daddy made to display them. I throw them down the slope of the front lawn. I run back two more times and drop pots over the side of the porch so that they make a delicious breaking noise on the cement floor like bones splintering.

Someone is enjoying this as much as I am. Someone is cackling.

The porch light blooms on Rosa Benson's porch, and soon she is standing there in her nightgown staring at me. I keep dancing and waving my arms and kicking pots onto the sidewalk. Rosa disappears into her house, but soon she is back and making her way to our house. Her arms are wrapped firmly in front of her, accentuating her breastless chest. Then she stands in front of our house on the sidewalk, looking up at me. I see all of this in my peripheral vision, because I am dancing and turning and swaying above her on the upper slope of the lawn. I only stop for a brief second, when Rosa Benson shouts my name in that voice that could halt the creation itself. I stop and turn and blink.

Her voice drops to a whisper, "Lord, child," she says. So there's another prayer in my behalf.

"I am not a child," I say, weaving down the slope to her. "I'm a woman. I'm having a baby, you know."

Finally I am standing right in front of her and I point at my face and my closed eye and say, "And this proves that it was immaculately conceived."

She touches my face so gently that I can't think about it. "Who did this to you?"

"I did it to myself." It isn't exactly a lie, if you think about it hard.

A siren wails up 8th South. Rosa Benson stiffens and turns her head to look for it as if she expects it to turn into our street. And it does—it's the paramedics. Their truck stops in front of our house.

Mama, clutching a hankie to her nose, peers through the living room window, her eyes red and wild.

"Help is here for you, Mama," I cry. "Help is here. Help is finally here," I say. I'm so relieved. Mama has needed help for years. I twirl on the upper slope of the lawn, my fingery branches twitching skyward.

The emergency team, a woman and a man, whisper with Rosa Benson. I sing a little song: "Everything will be fine, fine, fine! Didle, didle, die . . ."

Another siren. This time a police car pulls up behind the ambulance.

Mrs. Goodrow peeks through her window at us, her face pushed right against the glass, her hands curved around her eyes as if to protect them from sunlight. I see her at the same time I see the emergency workers coming up the lawn to get Mama, and I see Rosa Benson's pressed lips. I see Mama disappear from behind the window, the front door closes. I hear the lock. You can run, but you can't hide, Mama.

I see and hear everything as I sway my branches and kick up my roots. Perhaps I even see the policemen grab me from behind. I shove hard against them and they falter on the slope of the lawn. "Maybe we should use—" It's a male voice.

"I think so." Another male voice.

There is blood on my shirt. I want to wipe it off, but I can't move either arm. I'm handcuffed.

PART II

Trilby Speaks

You know how you think you're best friends with someone and then something happens and you realize maybe it was only *you* that thought you were best friends? Maybe your best friend doesn't think of *you* as *her* best friend? Get what I mean?

I've known Hannah all my life. We went to the same nursery school up at the Unitarian Church on 13th East, and we both went to Emerson School and had Ms. Nordvall in the morning kindergarten, who used to count the number of squares of toilet paper you used after you went to the bathroom. If you used more than six, she'd yell at you. Hannah and I played "O Holy Night" on violin and flute for the Christmas program at church when we were twelve. And that same year, Hannah wore a dress to school and her slip fell down in front of Mr. Peterson out on the playground. She picked it up and hid it behind her back. We laughed so hard, we wet our pants. Mr. Peterson said, "You don't have to be embarrassed, girls; I have daughters." Hannah can still do an imitation of him saying that in his high, nasal voice. "Can you imagine Mr. Peterson having sex?" she asked me.

I can't really imagine anybody—you know—doing it.

Hannah's pregnant, and she didn't even tell me. I found it out thirdhand. Rosa Benson told my mom and my mom told me. I went upstairs and sat on my bed looking out the window at the iris bed where Hannah and I buried my Barbie and Ken dolls when I got my first period. I had a dozen of those dolls. Sometimes I miss them and want to dig them up, but I'm afraid there'd be worms in the boxes. Hannah started her period a year before me. Now she's done *it* before me. And she's pregnant. How could she be pregnant?

My mom follows me up to my room and asks me if I knew that Hannah was having sex.

I shake my head. "I haven't seen her as much since she started dating Milo," I say. "He took up pretty much all her time."

Rosa Benson knows more than anyone, because she checks with the psychologists at the hospital for Hannah's mother, who doesn't like to call out on the phone. My mom says that if Mr. Ziebarth could see Mrs. Ziebarth now, he wouldn't recognize her.

I guess that's true. She has changed a lot, but even before he died, he made calls for her. He even made her appointments at the hairdresser. He and Hannah did most of the cooking. Although Mrs. Ziebarth made these fantastic alphabet cookies when she was room mother. Everyone wanted her to be their room mother. She was beautiful then, not quite as beaten-down looking as she is now.

Mr. Ziebarth was a crackup. He was a professional photographer, and once he did these pictures of Hannah and me and fixed it so our heads had the bodies of monkeys hanging from a tree. I still have a framed one in my bedroom. And when I slept over at Hannah's he'd do his Nat King Cole imitation. He'd sing "L is for the way you look at me," even sounding like Cole, but there the imitation ended. He danced on his toes with knees bent, looking like a real fruit loop. "O is for the only one I see." He'd wiggle both index fingers at us and bend forward. "Love was made for you and me." Then he'd wink fast as if he had a sudden tic. Hannah and I laughed so hard we'd get the hiccups.

My mom thinks I should go visit Hannah, and she calls the hospital about visiting hours, but Hannah can't see anyone. I'm relieved. I don't know what I'd say to her. It's like Hannah is an adult now, and I'm still a kid. It's like if I see her she'll be this stranger. I figure I can just write her a note, but when I try, all I can think of is, "Hope you're feeling better," with a lot of XOs after it. My head fills with questions I don't dare ask her: What is it like to have sex? What is it like to be pregnant? Did you have a nervous breakdown?

So I go to the What-Not Shoppe over on 9th South to buy a get-well card. Most of the cards are for old geezers, as if kids don't get sick. Finally I pick one that says:

Roses are red,
Violets are blue;
I've written a special poem for you . . .
Hope you feel better,
Hope you feel well.
Now get out of bed,
Your hair looks like Hell!

I put a lot of XOs after it and sign it, "Your friend, Trilby." Then I feel dumb that I wrote "Your friend," as if she didn't already know. How many Trilbys does she know? Your teacher, Trilby? Your grocery clerk, Trilby? Your insurance rep, Trilby? But I can't cross it out, because that's even dumber. I put the card in its yellow envelope and lick it shut. I don't want my mom to see it, because I know she'd think the card was "irreverent." She'd want me to buy a card with flowers and butterflies and gold curly cursive that says, "To a dear friend whose soul is like my own," or something equally gross.

My mom is in the kitchen sprinkling grated cheese over a casserole when I ask her for a stamp. "It's a card for Hannah," I say, waving it at her.

"Nice, honey. The stamps are in my bag—in the side pocket."

I find them, lick one, and set it in place. "I'm going to mail this," I say.

"Great," she says. And I escape. When I mail it at the corner, I feel good. I feel "mature," as my mom says. Hannah will know I don't think any less of her, and that I'm still her friend. The card says all that. Then too, it's now Hannah's turn to send *me* a letter or call me, or come by when she's out of the hospital, and maybe by that time I'll know what to say to her.

But on Monday, I come home from baby-sitting at the Wakefields' and my mom tells me that tomorrow we can visit Hannah at the hospital. She says I should buy her a present. Something nice, she says.

"Like what?" I say. I can't imagine what to buy a pregnant, mentally ill person. "You mean a present for the baby?"

My mom turns away from the chair she's painting and looks at me as if I've just turned back into a three-year-old. "No, Trilby—I mean a present for Hannah, a get-well present." She holds the paintbrush poised in the air. "Are you all right?"

"Yeah, I guess." I open the refrigerator and pull out a lemon yogurt. A get-well present? Hi, hope you get well soon from that pregnancy. Or even worse: hope you're back on your rocker soon.

"I don't want to visit the hospital." I speak softly into the yogurt carton, because I'm not sure if I want Mom to hear me.

She lays the brush on top of the paint can and stands up. "I know," she says.

"If it were her birthday, or Christmas, or graduation or anything, I'd know what to buy—"

"But this is more serious." Her hands are on my shoulders, but I can only stare into my yogurt.

"Mom, Hannah's always been the one who made *me*

laugh. I don't know how to be with Hannah when she's in this kind of trouble. I'm sure I'll say the wrong thing. I'm sure I'll make it worse." I start to cry like the big baby that I am.

Mom hugs me and rubs my back. "You'll think of something," she says. "Hannah just needs to know that you're still her friend."

"I don't know if I still am." I've said the worst, and my mom doesn't drop over dead or even wince.

"Then you'll find out tomorrow evening, when we go visit her."

"I'll get her some roses," I say. "Hannah's nuts about roses." And then catching myself, "I mean, she *loves* them."

Mom smiles. "I think *nuts* about covers it."

Later I walk down to 9th and 9th to the flower shop and look at the long-stemmed roses in the buckets outside the shop. Perfect roses, and perfectly alike. I bend to smell them and remember standing in front of roses just like these with Hannah. "They look like they've been stretched on the rack," she had said. "They look like they've been grown in molds, like they've been designed by mathematicians."

In that moment, I know what I probably have known all along: If I really want to make Hannah happy, I'll have to steal the roses.

I set my alarm for five the next morning, but either it doesn't go off or I punch it off in my sleep, because I don't wake up until seven-fifteen, which is way too late for stealing in our neighborhood. Everybody's up by then. In fact, while I'm brushing my teeth, I can hear Mr. Knight's backhoe sputtering in the distance. I don't bother to shower, but throw on my overalls over my nightshirt and put my dad's Utah Jazz cap on my head. Maybe if anyone sees me they'll think I'm my father.

Mom is in the kitchen when I pull a Thriftway bag out of the drawer and pull the scissors from the cup of pencils next to the microwave.

"I'm getting some roses for Hannah," I say, heading out the back door.

"That's nice, honey." The screen door bangs shut.

It won't count beans for Hannah if I cut roses from our yard, so I cut through the Wakefields' and pick the one blooming rose in the whole yard. The weather has been hot, so most of the roses are past the best bloom. This one's a beautiful yellow. Hannah would know its name, but I'm clueless. I'm placing it in the plastic sack when someone calls, "Good morning, Trilby," and it's Annie Wakefield, holding her new baby out on her screened porch. I about wet my pants but I manage a weak wave and I think I even smile. "Hi," I say, and walk on down the side of her house. Geez, I don't know why Hannah thinks this is so fun.

I pick off roses easily at the Masons', Walls', Strongs', and Keddingtons'. Now I am at Rosa Benson's. I'd rather skip her yard, but Hannah, I know, considers her roses the prize. Not because they're better than anyone else's but because Rosa Benson can be downright dangerous. Hannah says she's a witch and ate her husband at a Fourth of July picnic. Then she looked at the dog, their pet, Hannah claims, and said, "Everyone's eaten but you." It breaks Hannah up when she tells it.

My dad says Rosa's cranky because she's a Democrat in a Republican state and they're always feeling beaten down.

"The meaner the rose owner, the more valuable the rose, and Rosa Benson is the meanest." This is Hannah's philosophy.

I'm in Hannah's backyard now, looking over the fence into Rosa's back window. I see nothing and open the gate, which creaks like something out of a Halloween movie. Still nothing.

I cut the roses nearest the gate, crouching down as low as I can, and slip them into the bag. I must have two dozen roses now and I hope that Hannah is well enough to appreciate this feat of friendship. I'm almost finished when I see the most beautiful lavender rose. I've never seen a rose this color, and I get on my knees and crawl over to it, because it's close to Rosa's kitchen window. The lawn is wet and cool on my knees. I glance up at the window. She's not looking out. In fact, I'm beginning to doubt that she's even home.

Hannah will be so proud of me. Once when I had slept over at her house, I went out with her on her early-morning rose hunt, but I wouldn't step off the sidewalk into anyone's yard. "It's immoral to steal," I said. I could tell my voice sounded prissy.

"Yeah, sure." She clipped a couple of roses out of Mrs. Keddington's front yard.

"Any of these people would gladly let you clip a few roses if you asked them, so what's the point?"

She looked up at me then, her eyes squinting from the sun beyond my shoulder. "The point is that I'm not living my life anymore by somebody else's rules." She sounded mad, but then, catching herself, she lightened up and said, "Besides this is more fun." She turned back to her roses. "You can stay on the straight-and-narrow sidewalk if you want."

How did Hannah do that? How did she make me feel guilty for *not* stealing roses with her?

Well, I'm not standing on the sidewalk now. I'm in Rosa Benson's yard, chucking a lavender rose into my Thriftway bag.

"What do you think you're doing?" If a grizzly bear could speak, this is what she'd sound like. It's Rosa Benson and she's pointing a rifle at me.

"Nothing!" It comes out in a high screech. I clutch the bag of roses and scramble to my feet. "Honest." Hannah's inside my head grinning and chanting, "Liar, liar, pants on fire."

"You were stealing my roses." The rifle is aimed at my heart.

"No," I'm bleating. "No, I was just walking through and I dropped a contact lens." I point the sack of roses at the ground and then, realizing it's evidence, I hide it behind my back. "Don't shoot me. Please don't shoot me."

She lowers the gun. "Oh, keep your pants on," she growls. "This is just a BB gun—doesn't even hurt sparrows."

"It could put my eye out." I feel more confident now that the gun is pointing at the ground.

"Oh, don't be such a fool, girl." She wipes her forehead with the sleeve of her shirt. "Has Hannah started some kind of rose-stealing gang or something? I thought the garden was safe now that she's in the hospital, but it"—she gestures at the roses behind my back—"it seems to be escalating."

I shake my head. "No, I'm visiting her tonight, and I thought she'd like some roses—she likes them better if—"

"I know exactly what Hannah likes." Possibly there is a smile on her lips, but I'm not sure.

"Grandma!" a boy's voice calls from the side of the house. "Grandma, are you back there?"

"I'm here, Bradley." She turns sideways and waits for him to come into view. "Hi, darling," she says when he kisses her. I can hardly believe that Rosa Benson said the word "darling."

Bradley is my age, maybe a little older, and he's a babe. He's wearing denim shorts and a white T-shirt, his hair is more red than blond, like mine, and he's sunburned all over, especially his nose, which is peeling. I wish I'd showered before I came out.

"This is my grandson, Bradley," Rosa says with her hand on his shoulder.

"Brad, actually." He nods at me. "Brad Benson." He bites his bottom lip when he smiles.

"Hi. Trilby Evans." I think I'm dancing lightly on my feet, but I don't seem to be able to stop.

"She lives up on the next block but lost her contact lens in my yard." Rosa smirks.

"Oh, really?" He steps back as if it's under his foot and begins searching the ground.

"No, no." I laugh nervously. My hand flutters toward Rosa. "She's kidding. She's—"

He smiles widely this time. "Yeah, she does that." And then, noticing the gun, he says, "Is this it?" He takes it and rubs the shiny wood handle, then aims it into Hannah's yard. "It's a beauty," he says. "It really is."

Rosa is obviously glad that he likes it, but she says, "I don't think the thing even shoots, but you can fiddle around with it. Do what you want."

"Thanks, Grandma. I'll take it up to the cabin this weekend and see if I can fix it."

"Don't shoot out your eye." I can't believe I've said this. I try to fix it. "Or you can if you want." I shrug.

"Thanks." He grins.

Rosa grabs the bag of roses out of my hands. "I'll put these in water before they wilt in this sun." She pulls out an old coffee can from under the porch and turns on the hose. I am left standing alone with Brad, anxious about making conversation.

"So where's your cabin?" I ask. It's lame, but I can't think of anything else.

"It's up on the Bear River not far from Preston, Idaho. Do you know where that is?"

"Yes, I do. My grandpa's farm is right on the Bear River—on the west side."

"You're kidding. That's real close to our place."

Rosa has arranged the roses in the coffee can. It is an exquisite bouquet of just-opening blooms. "If this doesn't cheer her up, nothing will." Rosa Benson smiles at me when she hands them over. A real smile.

And I smile back. She is Brad Benson's grandma. What could be bad about her?

"I better be going," I say, and head for Hannah's gate.

"Hey, what's your grandpa's name?" Brad calls.

"Heber Evans," I say. "Everybody knows him."

"I'll come find you and we can go riding or something."

"Great," I say. "See ya."

"See ya."

Maybe Hannah's right. If you don't get off the straight-and-narrow sidewalk, nothing good ever happens to you. After all, I meet Brad Benson while stealing roses. There must be a fallacy here, but I don't really want to think about it.

Mom and I wait for Hannah in a room with two banquet-sized tables and folding chairs around them. There's a blackboard on one wall and it has notes about *The Scarlet Letter* written on it. My legs are crossed, and my foot twitches nervously back and forth, so that the roses on my lap flop about. I can't stop, though. The security for the adolescent unit of the hospital unnerves me. This room has a window with metal mesh running through it. It's like Hannah's in prison.

My mom must feel the same way because she's drumming a finger on the wrapped shoe box sitting on the table. It's a second gift for Hannah. I thought of it later in the day. The gift makes me nervous too. Maybe it's a bad idea. Mom smiles at me and whispers, "It'll be okay," but I think she's just trying to set an example. I wonder if Hannah will be wearing a hospital gown and slippers. I wonder if she had to be in a straitjacket.

Hannah appears in the doorway, a nurse behind her. "Hi," Hannah says. I see everything at once: the purple-and-yellow bruise on the side of her face and a smaller cut on the other side, the familiar shorts and shirt, the sandals, her bony frame. She doesn't *look* pregnant. Maybe she's not. Maybe it's all just a rumor.

"Hi," I say back. I try to smile. I try to stand. I feel like I'm suspended in Jell-O.

But my mom is quick. She's crossed the room by the time I stand and has her arms around Hannah. She holds her tightly, and I can see Hannah's eyes close against my mom's neck as if she feels safe for the first time in a long time. She clutches her as if she doesn't want her to stop the hug too soon, but my mom isn't going anywhere. My mom is a good hugger. She doesn't pat Hannah's back and treat her like some pet mouse.

It isn't until Hannah whispers, "I'm pregnant, you know," into Mom's shoulder that I realize she's crying.

Mom kisses her cheek. "I know," she says, "and it's going to be all right." She kisses Hannah again. They stand pressed together for a long time.

I feel too young to be here. I feel sheepish and on the outside of things. I feel jealous.

When they finally part, Hannah wipes her face with

the palms of her hands. She sees me, says "Hi" again and smiles broadly.

"I brought you roses," I say, holding them up. I hug her with my other arm.

She takes the vase of roses and buries her nose in them. "They're glorious. Oh my, yes." She cups them with her fingers and that's when she sees the lavender rose. "I didn't know you had an Intermezzo in your yard."

"They're not from our yard. None of them." I am so excited to be able to tell her this.

"But—"

"I *stole* all of them." I don't look at Mom's reaction.

Hannah's mouth falls open and she lets out a screech. "This is Rosa Benson's Intermezzo?"

"Yes. And she caught me stealing it. She pointed a rifle at me!"

Both of us screech then and laugh. "In fact, I got caught by just about everybody."

"You stole roses for me? You, Trilby-stand-on-the-sidewalk-and-whimper-Evans, stole roses for me? Are you a friend or what?" She puts her arm through mine and giggles. "I love it. I really love it."

"I'm glad," I say.

I had forgotten about the nurse in the doorway, but now she comes forward and says, "Let me put these in a plastic container for you."

I am surprised since the roses are already in a nice glass vase, but Hannah hands them over to her.

"I'll put them in your room, okay?" the nurse says.

Hannah smiles and nods. "They won't let us have glass in here," she whispers to Mom and me, "because some of the kids are suicidal." She makes a large grimace. "Not only is she going to put them in an ugly plastic pitcher, but she's also going to take all the thorns off them. Some of the kids here like to cut themselves." Her hand reaches up to touch the small cut at the side of one eye and then quickly withdraws to her side.

"Geez," is all I can say.

"No kidding." Hannah grins. "I'm the sanest person here by a long shot. Now, *that's* scary!" She laughs.

Mom smirks at the two of us. "I'm going for a little walk and let you two talk," she says. "I'll be back in a while." She blows Hannah a kiss and disappears.

"Here, I got you another present," I say, and lead her to the table, where we both sit down.

Hannah picks up the box and shakes it lightly. "Goody," she says.

She looks so excited that I get nervous. "It's kind of a joke," I say. "Maybe it's not even funny—"

"What is it? Birth control?" She laughs at me, unwrapping the box. She lifts the lid, blinks at the contents, takes it out and squeals: "A pregnant Barbie! A very pregnant Barbie! My gosh, where did you get this?"

I can relax now, because I see that she loves it. "Look under the dress," I say.

She pulls the dress up and guffaws. I have taped a tiny rubber baby upside down on Barbie's tummy. "I made the maternity dress myself," I say. "I'll make you one exactly like it when you need it."

She hugs the doll to her chest. "Remember when we buried all your Barbies and Kens?"

I can see that she's caught between laughing and crying, and I begin to wish my mother hadn't left. It is easier when Hannah's laughing. "I remember," I say.

"I could use a Ken right now." A kind of half sob, half laugh escapes her mouth.

I don't know what to say, how to look. "I'm sorry," I say finally. I've never seen anyone look so sad. No one our age should be this sad, I think.

"Well." She literally shakes off the sadness. "Tell me about stealing the coveted Intermezzo out of Rosa Benson's garden. I want to hear every detail."

This I can do, and I tell it to effect. Hannah is thrilled with the rifle part of the story. And when I tell her about meeting the fabulous Brad Benson and how he's going to look me up, she squeezes my hand and says, "I'm taking full credit for this. If it weren't for me, you'd never have met him. Give me full credit. Give me."

I give her a high five.

We sit in silence for a minute. Should I ask her what I want to ask her? "Rosa Benson thinks that it's Milo who beat you up. Is that true?" I need to know for sure.

She nods.

"What a creep," I say.

Hannah nods doubtfully. "I guess," she says.

"You're not sure?" She's so unusually passive that I'm shocked.

"Yeah," she says slowly, "I guess he is a creep. It's hard. He was so nice for a long time. Wasn't he nice?"

"Yeah—no. I don't know. I always think that really good-looking people should be nice too. I don't know him, really. He never talked to me."

"He didn't?"

I shake my head. "Even after the two of you started dating he never said hello in the halls. I don't think he even knows who I am." She stares straight at the black-board, at *The Scarlet Letter*, scrawled in chalk.

"He knows who you are. I used to talk about you all the time. He saw us together. He even ate lunch with us a couple of times. Remember?"

"He never talked to me," I say. "Honest."

Hannah still looks confused when the nurse comes in. "Visiting hours are over," the nurse says.

Hannah stands up immediately. "I have to go. I can't afford to lose points." She hugs me quickly. "Thanks for the wonderful stolen roses. It takes my breath away to think you did that for me. And thanks for pregnant Barbie. This is one Barbie that will never be buried." She giggles.

"We'll come again," I say, and I mean it. "Love you."

"Love you too."

We both step out of the room. I watch her walk down the hall past the nurses' station. She turns once and waves at me with the Barbie. I wave back and go to meet my mom.

That night I can't sleep. I keep thinking of my mom holding Hannah in her arms and telling her everything will be all right. I think of her kissing Hannah's face.

Finally I get out of bed and go downstairs. I walk through the dark kitchen and out onto the screen porch. "Mom?"

She is standing in her robe looking out over the garden, and she turns when I call to her. "Can't you sleep either?" she says to me.

"I was thinking of Hannah," I say, even though it's only half true.

"Me too," she says. We stand next to each other looking at the stream of moonlight cutting across the lawn and listening to the crickets. I can smell my mother's hand lotion and perfume. She has worn the same scent all my life.

"Mom." There's an unexpected catch in my voice, but I continue: "If I got pregnant, would you hug me the way you hugged Hannah tonight? Would you kiss my face and tell me everything would be all right?"

She turns then and looks into my face as if she's seeing me for the first time. "Oh, darling, yes!" Then she draws me in and we are pressed together. "If I have taken you for granted, I am so sorry," she whispers, and kisses my cheek. "You're everything I ever wanted in a daughter. Everything."

Seeing Hannah tonight, I realized that the world may be a dangerous place, but for the time being, I hold on to my mother and feel safe to be her child.

PART III

Hannah Speaks

I will not speak. Not in English, not in French, not in Guacamole. Language stinks. Lie, and people believe you. Tell the truth, and they don't. While I count to ten by twos, guess what these people have in common: Mama, Mrs. Goodrow, Mr. Knight, and Milo Fabiano.

Time's up. Here are hints: Mama hasn't left the house in two years, not to hear me play in the orchestra or attend a back-to-school night, not to have lunch with a friend or buy herself a dress, not to the grocery store, not to church, which she says she's devoted to. She hasn't made a phone call. Mrs. Goodrow dates her checks 1935, the year she got married, and uses Easter seals as postage. She is often seen walking down the sidewalk in her nightgown or slip. Mr. Knight digs craters into perfectly flat lawns with his backhoe and piles up mountains of dirt in the front yards of his rental properties. Milo Fabiano "exhibits violent behavior." The quote is from *my* medical chart, not his, *because he isn't in here.* None of them is in here. Get it? They're crazy, but they're not in here. Go figure. How come I'm in here and they're not? Who gets to decide who's crazy?

The psychologist does, for one. She comes to see me at intervals. She brings a chair with her and sits close to my bed and calls me by name: "Hannah?"

Even though I won't look at her, I see the nameplate she wears on the lapel of her jacket: Caitlin Saunders, Ph.D., Adolescent Unit. I've given up spoken language, pointless as it is, so I don't answer.

"Do you know why you're here?"

Yes. What I don't know is, why aren't there a half dozen people in here with me?

"Do you remember the paramedics bringing you in?"

The *police.* In handcuffs, like I was a criminal. The language in my head is impossible to stifle now. I try to think of something neutral to drown out her voice, her soft voice. Bricks. Bricks. Bricks.

"Do you remember having your head stitched?"

Bricks. Bricks. Bricks.

"Do you remember kicking the nurse?"

Did I kick a nurse?

"I talked to your mother this morning and she says to tell you not to worry about her—that the people at church are taking good care of her. Hannah?"

I kicked a nurse?

"It's all right. You don't have to talk if you don't want to. I'll just sit here awhile with you."

I don't remember kicking a nurse.

She reaches over and pushes my bangs back from my face like Daddy used to do. I won't think about that. She sits with me in silence for an hour. Or fifteen minutes. I have time to see that she is younger than any doctor I've ever had before. That she has a light birthmark on her wrist. I have time to sense that the silence doesn't make her nervous, that her posture is relaxed in the chair, that she breathes evenly. I try to match my breath with hers. When she leaves, I miss her.

I sleep without dreams. I wake without hope. Sleep is better. Sleep.

Another time, I remember something—something I learned in health class—and I am angry. I sit at the edge of the bed waiting for her, rocking myself back and forth. Rock rock rock. If I stop rocking I will explode all over the room.

Dr. Saunders arrives, again carrying a chair, which she sets in front of me. When she is seated, I stand up. I don't want to see her even in my peripheral vision. I pace back and forth in front of the door. If I watch the floor I won't see the delicate birthmark, the way her hands fold into her lap.

I will wait for her to speak, so that I can interrupt her. I will be rude.

Why doesn't she speak?

I begin to puff and cross my arms in front of me, burying my fists under my armpits. Tension knots my upper arms, my shoulders, the back of my neck. The face of a nurse appears in the little window in the door, and I smash my fist sideways against the glass. "Let me out of here!" I yell. I turn on Dr. Saunders. "It's against the law to hold me here." My voice is shrill and breathy. It's not the way I want to sound. I want to sound cold and rude and superior with my knowledge about my constitutional rights. "You can't institutionalize a person against her will. It's Utah law." My voice shakes.

"That's true." Her head nods. "An adult cannot be held longer than seventy-two hours against her will, and even then, there needs to be evidence that the patient might endanger others or herself."

Even though she doesn't emphasize the word "adult," it echoes inside my head. I hear a big "but" coming.

"But," she says just like I knew she would, "that's not true with minors. The law gives parents blah, blah . . . pish, pish . . . , and your mother signed the papers."

Mama signed papers? I turn and look at Dr. Saunders for the first time. "Mama came to the hospital?"

"No." She looks straight into my eyes. "She had a neighbor of yours take the papers to her and return them."

I can't read her look or her voice. Does she feel sorry for me? I look away from her. "That would be Rosa Benson," I whisper. "She'd sign me in here herself if she had half a chance."

Dr. Saunders says that it was a Mrs. Benson.

"I want to call Mama," I say, taking a step toward her. "I want to talk to Mama."

She nods. "You can after you've completed your orientation. Do you feel up to doing that today?"

"Can't I talk to her now? I just need a few minutes."

"After orientation."

I want to scream at her and make her take me to a phone. I want satisfaction. I struggle with this urge, knowing it won't get me anything but another day in this room. How many days have I been here? Finally I say, "What do I have to do?"

Dr. Saunders stands and walks over to me. She holds my arm lightly above the elbow and says, "First, let's get you out of here and into a better room." She is shorter than I am, and when she opens the door I get the idea that I could flatten her and make my escape, but when we step into the hallway I am overwhelmed by the nurses' unit across from us, the bright sunlight coming through the window at the end of the hall, and the exits on all sides leading to who knows where. And then too, I wonder if I really am crazy. I decide to stay long enough to figure out where the exit is.

Dr. Saunders introduces me to a squat nurse named Nancy, who, she says, will see me through the orientation. Nancy hands me a yellow booklet. "This tells you about the rules," she says. "You can read it after breakfast. First let me show you to your room." I follow her past the large window, which has a wire mesh running through it. Bars of the nineties, I guess. "This is the girls' hall," she tells me. "On the other side of the window down that way is the boys' hall. You aren't allowed in that hall and vice versa." I don't see anyone my age and wonder if I'm the only person in the unit.

As if she reads my mind, she says, "The kids have all

gone with a couple of counselors on a Fourth of July picnic. You'll meet them later."

"Today's the Fourth of July?" I ask.

She nods.

Somewhere I have lost two days.

We pass a couple of bedrooms and then go into the one at the end of the hall. It is larger than the time-out room and has two single beds in it and a two-sided desk with a chair on each side. Over one bed there are two posters taped to the wall: one of Sting and one of Burpee's Oriental Poppy Seeds. I must have a roommate. Where is she? There's also a wire-mesh window overlooking a side parking lot and an old neighborhood beyond that. Something is funny about the mirror on the wall, but I don't have time to figure it out, because Nancy has taken a suitcase out of the closet. I recognize it as one of Daddy's. "Here are some clean clothes for you. Why don't you pick out something and then you can take a shower."

My clothes are methodically packed inside the suitcase, socks rolled neatly into one corner. A small bouquet of dried roses tied with ribbon lies on top of everything. They are from the nightstand in my room at home. I lift them out carefully.

"What's that?" Nancy is by my side.

"Dried roses," I say. They are Queen Elizabeths, but I don't say this.

"Let me see." She takes the roses from me and looks them over carefully. "They don't seem to have any thorns," she says.

"I remove the thorns before I dry them," I tell her.

She scrutinizes them again. "I guess they're okay." She hands them back to me. "Can't kill yourself with those."

"Kill myself?" I say.

"You'd be surprised what some kids have tried." She shakes her head.

I lay the dried roses on the desk and pick a T-shirt at random. It says "U.S. Soccer Association" on the front of it. I hide the shirt under the other clothes and pick another.

The shower room is communal, with half a dozen stalls in it and as many sinks against one wall. A mirror runs across the whole wall above the sinks, and now I see what's odd about the mirror. It is the same as the one in my room. Instead of glass, it is made of a molded aluminum. My image takes me by surprise, the hair matted and oily.

The shower is lukewarm and I wash quickly. While I'm dressing, Nancy reminds me to use the toilet because I'm not allowed in the bathroom for an hour after I eat.

"I've used it," I say.

I eat breakfast in the dining room, which is also the schoolroom. Nancy sits with me with her clipboard and pen, and when I shove my tray aside, she asks if I'm finished.

I nod.

She shakes the orange juice carton. "Good," she says, "You drank it all." She checks out the cereal bowl, which is mostly empty, and seems pleased. "Aren't you going to eat any toast?" she asks.

"I'm not that hungry," I say.

"Well, I think that's about seventy percent." She jots it down onto the page on the clipboard and then tells me to do the same on the daily record in the orientation book, which I do.

After breakfast, I'm left with the yellow booklet, which explains the program. I learn from it that while we are here we have to attend school in the morning. That I have individual therapy, group therapy, recreational therapy, and—this kills me—*family* therapy. According to the booklet, my *family* will come in twice a week to have therapy with me. I lay my head down on my folded arms on the desk. To get my family to this hospital would require a raising of the dead and enough Xanax to kill a cow.

"It will have to be you and me, baby of mine," I whisper. "You and me in family therapy."

When Nancy returns, I probably look like I'm asleep. "Have you read the rule book?" She looks at me suspiciously.

I raise my head and nod.

She reaches into some papers on her clipboard. Her blouse rises up while she's searching for the right sheet and I see that her pants are held shut with a safety pin. She hands me a quiz on the orientation booklet and a pencil and then stands behind me while I take the quiz.

I know about visiting hours from six to seven each night, but I can't remember what they are on Sundays, or what times I'm allowed to make phone calls. But Nancy corrects it and tells me I passed. "Good," she says. "You can mark that in your daily diary. I mark it. "Good," she says again. I feel like I'm in nursery school.

"Okay, now I'll take you down to pediatrics for a physical exam and then we'll come back here and you can take the MMPI." She shoves the quiz I've just taken in with the papers in her clipboard.

I stand up to follow her.

"You're wearing a belt!" Her fat, dimpled hand covers her mouth. She is as shocked as if I were carrying an automatic weapon. "When did you put that on?"

"When I got dressed." I can't understand her problem.

"I didn't even see it." She starts tugging at the belt. "You'll have to take it off."

The belt is a Native American belt that Daddy bought for me in Southern Utah—silver medallions with turquoise studs in them. "Wait, you'll break it," I say. She's pulling at the front of it.

"It clips in the back," I tell her. I reach back and undo it.

She pulls it through the belt loops frantically and dumps the belt, which jingles, in a pile on top of her clipboard. "No belts," she says. "Belts aren't allowed."

When we're out in the hall, she deposits the belt in a box behind the nurses' station. "You can have it back when you leave," she says.

"And when will that be?" I ask.

"That'll be up to you."

She pisses me off.

The physical exam mainly consists of peeing in a cup and a blood test. Easy. But the MMPI is irritating. It's this psychological test that asks the same questions over and over again, trying to catch you in a lie. Like it wants to know if my stools are blacker or softer or more frequent than other people's stools. After the third stool question, I write in the margin, "Who cares about stupid stools?"

On my way to lunch, Dr. Saunders meets me in the hallway. "Would you like to call your mother now? You can do it in my office."

I nod and follow her into a small, neat room behind the nurses' station. I am satisfied to see that the one window has the wire mesh running through it. Dr. Saunders is also a prisoner. Next to the phone is a tiny pot of miniature roses, a present, judging from the shiny paper and white ribbon around the pot. "This should be in the window," I can't help saying. "Roses need lots of sunlight."

"Oh," she says, and moves the pot to the windowsill.

It needs repotting too, but I don't say this. Roses don't really belong inside. Miniature roses are an abomination. I can't remember the name of this one. I pick up the phone and dial. It rings a long time. Has Mama now stopped answering the phone?

Finally, it's picked up. "Mama?"

"Hannah, is that you?"

"I was afraid you wouldn't pick up."

"Are you okay? I was so worried about you."

"I'm fine now." I turn to look at Dr. Saunders to see if she would agree, but her back is turned toward me; she's looking out the window. "I'm a lot better," I say.

"Oh, I'm so relieved. You scared me to death—"

"Well, it's all right. I'm better, really—"

"The way you threw all my pots around—"

"Yeah, but—"

"It was like you were mad at *me*!" Her voice is filled with surprise.

"No, that wasn't it—"

"But you know what? I was able to save every single plant, although some of them had to be trimmed down, because of broken branches. You know how fragile they are. And everyone has been so kind—people from the church bring me plates of food and Rosa Benson sees to it that I have plenty of plants to work on during the day—"

"Mama, listen!" I try to control my agitation. "I want to come home now." I don't mean to sound so abrasive and try to calm my voice. "Make them let me go. You can sign me out."

"Oh, Hannah—" Her voice cracks.

"Please, Mama."

"But Rosa says it will take two or three weeks before you're stabilized. She used to be a nurse, you know."

"I don't give a shit. She's not my mother. You're my mother!"

"Oh, don't say that terrible word. I hate that word." She's crying.

"Shit. Shit. Shit!"

"Hannah, I can't listen—" She hangs up.

I raise the phone and smash it into the desk, shattering the earpiece. I can't stop saying the word my mama hates. Then I remember the name of Dr. Saunders's miniature rosebush: Bit o' Magic.

I'm not a good mental patient. I'm not a good daughter. I'm not a good Christian. Not a good student. Not a good flute player. Not a good girlfriend for Milo Fabiano—not careful enough. Probably won't be a good mother either. Baby, Baby, how can I keep you and be your mama? Already I love you. How can I not be your mama? I rock back and forth on the bed. I cry over Baby. I cry over me.

When I get out of isolation, I meet my roommate, who sits at one side of the desk painting her fingernails black. "Poppy Seed," she says. It takes me a second to realize that she's introducing herself. Her hair is magenta and her face is a masterwork of silver studs—nose, eyebrows, lips, ears—a stud gun run amok.

"I'm Hannah," I say. "Hannah Ziebarth."

"Zeeee-barff?" A corner of her upper lip rises to a sneer.

I stare at her. "Whatever." I've seen girls like her standing in front of the downtown Nordstrom pestering passersby for handouts.

She surprises me, though: "Just kidding." She looks up for the first time. "Really." Her hands flutter into the air and she blows on her fingernails, which are bitten to the quick. "Want me to do yours? I'm really careful." The plea in her voice doesn't match her heavy-metal exterior.

I nod and sit opposite her at the desk and spread my fingers out on the fake wood surface.

"You have a choice," she says. "Black or"—she brings up another bottle of polish hidden in a rolled-up sock in the drawer—"or black!"

"I think I'll try black." I point at one of the identical bottles. "I thought we weren't supposed to have glass around," I say, nodding at the bottles of lacquer.

She swings the sock at me. "That's why we have these!" Her smile bares a set of tiny teeth with spaces between them. Baby teeth. She unscrews a lid and begins working on my thumb, biting her lip as she works. She does have a steady hand. I wonder what Mama would say about black fingernails.

"Why are you here?" she asks.

No one has asked me this. Everyone until now seems to know why I'm here, but I don't. I stammer, "I—I, that is, my mother signed me in." This is not an answer, I realize, so I say, "I'm crazy, I guess," and then add, "I had this huge fit on the front lawn and the neighbors called the police."

"Is that how you hurt your eyes?" She touches the scar with the swollen bruise. "Geez, you've got about eight stitches in there. Does it hurt?"

"Not anymore."

"You look like you spent the night in a hotel room with Mike Tyson."

I nod. Milo is not like Mike Tyson. He wouldn't hurt anyone.

He hurt you.

I try to shake the thought out of my head, glad that Poppy Seed, or whatever her name is, likes to talk.

"I'm a drunk," she says. "If I don't dry out this time, they'll take my baby away from me."

"You have a baby?"

"Yeah, you want to see pictures?" Without waiting for an answer, she digs into a black leather bag and brings out a small photograph album. She holds on to it while showing me the snapshots. "He's a boy—ten months old. Cute, isn't he?"

"He's darling," I say. He already has a silver stud in one ear. His two teeth look just like hers. "I can't believe you have a baby."

"His name is Sting. I haven't had a drink for six weeks. That's the longest I've ever gone. Six freakin' weeks. I'm doin' it for you, hon." She places a black lipstick kiss on one of the pictures, wipes it with her finger, and sticks the whole book back into her bag. "I love Sting more than anything on Earth and he loves me more than anything."

Is she talking about the baby or the rock star?

She finishes painting my nails. "Here, put this on so you match." She hands me her lipstick. I stand in front of the molded aluminum mirror and put it on. I am pale and the black lipstick makes me look like I have a dark gash in my face. Strangely, I like it.

"Your hair needs more poof." Poppy is already backcombing my hair. It stands out from my head in gauzy peaks.

A buzzer rings.

"That's the dinner bell." Poppy throws the comb on the bed. "Come on, I can't afford to lose any more points." She rushes out of the room. My electrically charged hair doesn't pat down easily and I am forced to go to dinner looking like some powerless Medusa.

Heads turn when I follow Poppy into the dining room.

"Oh my god, she's reproducing!" a skinny kid cries.

"Shut up, you fa—" Poppy stops when she sees the nurse, Nancy, placing dinner trays in front of the seated kids. Name-calling is against the rules. Nancy gives her a mild evil eye and looks suspiciously at my mouth and nails. Poppy and I sit together at the end of the table. There's about eight kids there, three boys. There's a blackboard on one side of the room with "Hester Prynne" scrawled across it and an upright piano in the corner. "This is also where we have school," Poppy whispers to me. She nods at Hester Prynne's name. "We're reading *The Scarlet Letter* right now. Have you read it?"

I shake my head.

"I hate that book, but I saw the movie with Demi Moore. She's cool."

Dinner is lasagna. It looks pretty good to me, but one of the girls pries at it with her fork. "I can't eat all of this cheese," she says. "Disgusting."

Nancy leans over her and pats her shoulders, encouraging her. She takes the fork from the girl and puts a little food on it and tries to coax her to eat it, but the girl turns her head, grimacing. Nancy replaces the fork next to her plate and says, "Do the best you can." The girl eats a piece of lettuce from the salad and a tiny piece of garlic bread. "I'm too full to eat all of this," she says.

"That's Brenda," Poppy whispers. "She's got eating disorders you've never even heard of."

It's hard to tell how thin Brenda is, because she's wearing layers of clothes. On purpose, probably. "She's really sick!" Poppy taps her forehead with an index finger. "I'd rather be a drunk."

"I'm the sickest one here, though," the boy on the other side of Poppy says. "I'm certifiably schizophrenic. I'm the only psychotic in the place."

"Yeah and you talk with your mouth full too. Gross. This is Axel," Poppy says. "This is Hannah."

"I've tried to kill myself twice," Axel says. He holds up his wrists. Both of them have scars.

"He thinks he's cured and then he stops taking his medication," Poppy explains to me. "I wish they had medication for drunks."

Axel holds his hands up in front of his face and rocks slowly in his seat. "The medication is so terrible. It makes me feel like somebody else."

"Maybe that somebody else is really you." Poppy elbows him.

Axel turns to me. "Why are you here?" As soon as he

asks, the other kids stop eating and wait to hear the answer.

I still don't know. "I'm not sure," I say.

"Who hit you?"

"A boy."

"Of course," two girls say together.

"You're probably depressed out of your mind," Axel says. "What have they got you on?"

Something in the morning. Something in the evening. Something pink. Something white. "I don't know," I say.

"Depression for sure," Axel says.

"And anxiety," says a girl.

"Maybe," I say. "I kicked a nurse, but I don't remember doing it."

A general howl goes up along with some feeble applause. Even Brenda smiles. "I guess I'm crazy," I say.

"Go for it!" a boy with glasses says.

But *crazy*, I know, is a child's word. I want a real label for what's wrong with me. Everyone else has a label: Eating disorder, substance abuse, bipolar disorder, schizophrenia—although I don't want *that* label. Surprisingly, I can think about it without lumps sprouting in my throat. I realize then that I haven't had trouble breathing or a lumpy throat since I was hospitalized. I decide to ask Dr. Saunders about this.

Over the next few days, Poppy becomes my mentor, reminding me who is who: Axel; Stephen; Link Bailey, a stoner who's been here once before, and who, for some reason, everyone calls by both first and last name: Lisa;

Denay; and Brenda. Poppy tells me that the reason we can't go to the bathroom for an hour after meals is so we can't throw up our food. *"Everyone* is bulimic!" She whispers this to me even though we're alone in our room. She tells me how to survive group therapy: "Just tell little stories about yourself—unimportant tidbits—then it seems like you've done your bit and they leave you alone."

She is also my hair artist, as she calls herself; this means my hair isn't the same style two days running. A lot of French braiding. When she suggests she could smuggle some dye in and make me a redhead, I decline.

She says she's being released any day now. I believe her.

One thing's sure. There is no stinking privacy in this place. I have therapy the afternoon after Trilby and her mother come to visit me and the first thing out of Dr. Saunders's mouth is, "I hear you had visitors last night. That's great."

Her cheerfulness pisses me off. I want to say what's so great about it. I want to say how would you like to collect crappy, good-goody family value points just so that you can have a visit with your best friend. I want to say why do you wear such stupid clothes—you always look like you're dressed in the Austrian national costume with those full skirts and that vest with the cutesy trim. I'm terrified you'll break into yodeling any minute.

"Your roses are dying," is what I really say.

She glances at the pot in the window. "Yes, they seem to be on their way out."

"They *do* need to be watered now and again," I say.

She leans forward in her chair so that her face is practically in mine. "So about the visit, Hannah, how was it?"

"You mean your little spies didn't tell you? Didn't the video cameras pick up our emotion-filled faces? The laughter and the weeping? Oh, you would have loved it!" I cock my head from side to side so she can get the full effect of the spikes Poppy teased into my hair this morning.

"Excuse me?"

"I mean aren't you just asking questions that you already know the answers to? Wouldn't our time be better spent learning a portable musical instrument or something—a mandolin? What do you think of the mandolin?"

Her lips press together in a fine line. Suppressed anger, I hope. Gotcha, Dr. Know-it-all.

"Why do you think you're reacting this way to my question?" Her voice is smooth, level. She isn't angry at all.

"Huh?" I grunt this.

She keeps those brown shiny eyes leveled at me. Waiting. She's wearing cowboy boots with the wide skirt. She doesn't look Austrian at all.

"Hannah?"

"What was the question?"

"Why do you think you're reacting—"

"I'm sick of this place, that's all. I'm sick of everyone spying on me and telling me when I can go to the bathroom and how much I can eat. I hate it here."

"So you're angry with the staff and me."

"Just because I got beat up, they bring me here. It's not fair." My voice no longer carries the earlier punch to it.

She bends forward in her chair. "You had a psychotic episode, Hannah. That's why you're here. Not because you got beat up."

Psychotic? "Is that what Rosa Benson said? Is it? She'd say anything to get rid of me." Psychotic?

She leans back in the chair now, her hands loosely folded in her lap. "Your mother *and,* yes, Mrs. Benson *and* the police *and* the emergency room staff all described your behavior. I'm the one who's calling it a psychotic episode."

"I'm psychotic?" I feel a rush of panic and clutch my middle. I rock in the chair. I know I'm doing it, but I can't sit still now. I'm psychotic and can't sit still. I rock. "Like Axel. I'm crazy like Axel?"

Dr. Saunders grasps my shoulder. "You're not schizophrenic." She shakes me a little. "You're not even psychotic. You had an *episode.* A single episode." She touches my cheek with her other hand. "That's why you're here—to find out why. And when you know why, you'll never have a repeat episode." She shakes me a little harder. "Hannah?"

It's clear to me now. I'm not normal and haven't been for some time. Maybe never. "I'll never be like other people again," I say aloud. "I'll never be normal."

Rock, rock, rock. "I saw it last night already." I hold myself tighter. "I'm so far from being like them."

"Who?"

"Trilby and her mother—they came. Trilby's mother hugged me and said I would be all right, and I felt safe for a minute. I felt so safe." I stop rocking. "And Trilby just takes that feeling for granted—that her mom will always be there fussing over her, making her keep appointments and do her homework and write thank-you notes . . ." I slump over and loosen the spikes in my hair so it falls forward over my eyes.

"Is that what normal is?" Dr. Saunders asks. "Feeling safe?"

I don't look up from under my hair when I nod.

"How long has it been since you felt 'normal,' as you put it?"

I can't remember the last time I felt normal. "I don't know," I say.

"Don't say you don't know so fast. Think. When was the last time you felt safe?" She waits. She's always willing to wait. Sometimes I hate that patient waiting.

Milo made me feel safe. Past tense.

I jerk up straight. "I'll tell you who *doesn't* make me feel safe: that freaking busybody, Rosa Benson." Her name explodes from my mouth. "It's her fault that I'm in this situation. She conned Mama into signing me in here—"

"Stop!" Dr. Saunders smacks the clipboard down into her lap. "Stop about Rosa Benson already!" She lowers her voice. "She is not the cause of your problems, Hannah." She pauses, searching for the right words. "You want to know something? All that anger at Rosa Benson keeps you from facing the real anger that you're too frightened to acknowledge." Her voice is gentle. "The truth is you'd rather have a psychotic episode than face all that anger. Who are you really angry with, Hannah? Because you can believe me on this one, it isn't Rosa Benson."

"You don't know anything," I say. It sounds feeble even to me.

"Well, if you'd stop blaming Mrs. Benson, I have a feeling other names would come to mind. Why don't you think about that—make a list."

I turn and look out the window, where it is a bright, sunshiny, click-your-heels kind of day. I can see the mountains off in the distance. The clock on her desk says that time is about up, and I say so: "Time to go!"

She looks at me, sadly, I think, but I don't care. I leave without saying good-bye.

She wants a list. Here's a list of people I'm angry with: Caitlin Saunders, Ph.D.; Nancy, the efficient day nurse; Jeanette, the efficient night nurse. That woman behind the desk who pushes the buzzer to let people in and out of the ward. Wes Jenkins, the other soggy therapist, who still wears jeans from the seventies and actually drinks chamomile tea from a mug, because it's good for his ulcer. Physician, heal thyself. I hate the whole crapload of them. More than anything I'd like to shoot Rosa Benson with her own gun for signing me in here.

———

The next evening, a new nurse pokes her head in the door. "You have a visitor," she says.

I think she is referring to herself, and I don't move from the bed. "Don't you want to come and see who it is?" She waves me into the hallway. "You can meet him in the classroom."

Him? I steady myself when I stand. Him? "A visitor for me?" I say. A *male* visitor for me, but I don't say that.

"You're a popular girl this week," she says referring to the visit from Trilby and her mom earlier in the week. She waits for me at the door.

I want to comb my hair; it's spiked in all directions, but don't think I should make her wait. I have a visitor and it's a "him." Milo? Milo come to say that it's all his fault, what a butthead he's been? Milo come to get me out of this place? He would get his own doctors. That's what Milo would do. Mrs. Fabiano would know a good doctor, probably one of her neighbors. Milo wants to make things better—I can forgive him. I *will* forgive him.

But it isn't Milo who has come to see me. It's Bishop Kelsey. Joke's on me. The next time someone asks me why I'm in here, I'll know what to say: delusional. *Chronically, incurably, fatally* delusional.

Bishop Kelsey stands by the blackboard next to Hester Prynne's name. He steps forward when he sees me. "Hannah," he says. A tiny flinch of the eyes tells me he's surprised by my ghoulish appearance. A look Poppy says makes me look "way cool."

"Hi, Hannah," he says, moving forward to shake my hand. "You're looking a little like one of the Talking Heads." He's wearing a dark suit.

"You're looking a little like an undertaker." I dare say this, because he was Daddy's friend before he was ever made bishop.

He smiles and leans forward. "It's my lawyer suit."

"And your bishop suit." I'm pretty sure he's here because he's my ecclesiastical leader, not because he's my lawyer.

He nods. "I'd feel better if this suit was lined in denim. He gestures for me to sit down at the table, and I do. He unbuttons his jacket and leans back in a chair facing me, his elbow resting on the table. "How are you doing?"

"I'm better now than I was when I came in here. You've probably already heard about that."

"Several versions."

"They're all true."

"I feel partly responsible," he says. "In fact, I owe you an apology, I think."

I don't know what I was expecting, but this wasn't it. "What?" I say. "Me? You haven't done anything."

"That's pretty much the point." He rubs the side of his face, searching for the right words. "When Brian—your dad—died, I knew your mother took it hard, and I knew she was generally anxious, but she kept coming to church and she said she was fine and that you were fine, and I believed her. Then she stopped coming to church. She said it reminded her too much of Brian, that it was too painful. I should have realized then that something was up." He looks disgusted with himself. "But whenever I came to visit, she really did seem fine; she was always animated and happy. She said a doctor was helping her with her fears and that as long as she was home, she managed . . ." He sighs. "Even her friends thought she was okay. We didn't realize . . ." His fingers rub the table surface. "We didn't realize that you were picking up so much slack. Way too much slack. I thought you bought groceries. I didn't realize you did everything else as well. These past few days I've had the Relief Society women bringing your mother breakfast, lunch, and dinner. She can't make a *sandwich.*"

"She can't set the table; she can't do her own laundry," I say.

"I'm just knocked over with the responsibility you've taken on, and I'm sorry I didn't recognize it and offer help a whole lot sooner." He leans forward. "I feel like I've let you down, Hannah." He clears his throat. "The church can continue helping with your mother's care forever if need be. I want to know how to help *you.*"

The only thing I can think of is new bras. My breasts are swollen because of the pregnancy, and my bras are too tight. I shake my head. Trilby and her mother can buy the bras. I can't even think of anything else. "I don't know," I say.

"What about legal counsel? I can help with that."

Why would I need legal counsel? I wonder.

He seems to read the question in my face. "You could bring a paternity suit against the child's father, you know."

"Oh, I couldn't—besides, I don't have any money—"

"Hannah, I don't want your money. I'd be happy to represent you in any way you need—pro bono—free." He stops; his face forms a grin. "Well, maybe a flute solo in church?"

"I guess I could afford that," I say.

He tells me other ways I might need an attorney, whether I decide to keep the baby or adopt it out. I'm relieved that he doesn't try to influence my decision either way.

He stands. "Is this place treating you okay?"

I nod.

"I'll check back with you in a few days, but if you need me before then, call me." He hands me a card. "Good-bye, Hannah."

I watch the bishop go down the hall past the nurses' desk. For a few seconds I feel lighter than I've felt for a long time. He came to apologize. When was the last time an adult did that? It's taking a whole bunch of women to fill in my job at home. Once I was strong. But the relief, the lightness quickly turns to a sour shame. How could Mama allow all those people to do things for her? How could she make us seem so desperate?

The night I am scheduled for family therapy, Dr. Saunders comes looking for me in my room. I'm sitting at the desk reading *The Scarlet Letter*, which is filled with people who need therapy worse than I do. What a spooky bunch.

"Hey," Dr. Saunders says, standing over me, "I have you scheduled for family therapy tonight. Don't you have it on your schedule?"

I close the book. "Yeah, but I don't have any family to come—I mean it would take a séance—I thought we'd just skip it."

She grins. "I have a plan. Come on."

I follow her to her office, relieved that she has not asked me about the list of people I'm angry with.

Instead of the usual two chairs facing each other, there are four chairs in a circle. The room feels crammed with furniture.

"Is Mama coming?" The possibility makes my voice squeak.

"She's coming in spirit only," Dr. Saunders says. She scribbles "Mama" with a thick black marker onto a piece of cardboard and sets it in one chair. "What did you call your father?" she asks, taking up another piece of cardboard.

"Daddy," I say. What is she doing?

She scribbles "Daddy" on the second piece of cardboard and sets it in the fourth chair. Then she sits down and turns to me. "As you know, Hannah, your mother is in no condition to come to the hospital, but she has agreed to meet with me in therapy twice a week . . ." She sees the bewilderment on my face. "I'll make house calls in her case." She smiles. "We're also going to evaluate her medications and see if something more helpful can't be done there."

"She takes Xanax," I say.

She nods. "Since she can't be here and since your father obviously can't be here, we're going to have to do something more creative in the way of family therapy for you—and maybe a little more difficult, but—"

"Dr. Saunders." I want to object before she even finishes.

"Call me Caitlin. Everyone else does."

I stare at the cardboard signs with the names I call my parents on them. This is so weird.

"Hannah? Did you hear me?"

"Yes—Caitlin—you want me to call you Caitlin."

"Good. Now, normally, you and your parents would be here and talk about any issues that you have with each other and I would be the facilitator, but since they can't be here, I want you to talk to the chairs as if they were your mama and your daddy."

"Talk to chairs? I can't do that. It's creepy."

"It sounds awkward, I know, but it works. Imagine your parents sitting there. Will you try?"

I shrug. "I guess."

"Now, the last time we were together, you were angry about being hospitalized—"

"Still am," I say.

"Maybe you could tell your mama how you feel about being here," she says.

I look at the chair and imagine Mama sitting there. It's not hard to imagine what she's wearing: a pair of dark slacks and a large shirt. It's her work outfit. Mama's lips are pressed together to hide the nervousness she feels about facing me in the room with a therapist present. She's as nervous as I am. Maybe more so. "Mama won't look at me. She's looking into her lap at her hands," I say.

"Tell her to look up," Caitlin urges.

I shake my head. "I don't want to talk to her."

"Talk to your dad, then."

I look at the other chair with Daddy's name in it and try to imagine him sitting there looking earnestly at me. He'd be busting his butt to help me. What was his face like? "I've forgotten his face," I cry, and cover my face with my hands.

Caitlin rubs my back. "What do you want to ask him? Try asking him a question."

"Daddy," I say, keeping my face covered. "Daddy, why did you die? Why? Everything's changed since you went. You shouldn't have died. Why did you?" I start to cry, thinking how miserable the last two years have been without him. How utterly sad not to have Daddy around.

Caitlin's voice is almost a whisper: "What does he answer?"

I look up at her. "Huh?"

"What's his answer? Go sit in his chair and answer the question." She nudges me with her hand, which is still on my back.

I do what she says and sit in Daddy's chair, holding the cardboard sign in front of me. I feel otherworldly, out of my own body.

Caitlin addresses me: "Brian," she says, "Hannah wants to know why you died and left her in such a difficult situation." She points to my old chair when she says my name. Then she waits for me to answer.

I know the answer, but I'm afraid to speak. Afraid my voice will come out sounding like Daddy's.

Caitlin nods for me to go ahead.

"I didn't want to die," I say. "It took me completely by surprise. I was in good shape, healthy, young." Daddy always worked hard at being fit. "It was one of those freak things. I didn't want to die. I wanted to be with your mom and see you grow up."

Caitlin motions for me to come back to my own chair, which I do. "What else do you want to know from him?" she asks.

"Does he know I'm pregnant?" I ask her.

"Ask him," she says.

I turn to the chair. "Do you know that I'm pregnant, Daddy?" I'm talking to a chair! This is not real, but Caitlin's face is serious, and she nods for me to continue. "I'm having a baby in January. I thought the father loved me, but he doesn't. I don't know what to do." I look down at the floor.

Without Caitlin's urging I move over to become my daddy. I think of how he must see me in the chair, my black fingernails, my poofy hair, my discolored face.

"Oh, Slim, you're so young."

I'm surprised to hear this come out of my mouth. I'd forgotten he called me Slim sometimes. I'd forgotten.

"I can't help you, baby, but you'll know what to do when the time comes. You're strong."

Without leaving the chair, but just by changing directions, I become Hannah. "No, I don't know what to do." My voice is angry. "I want to keep the baby, but Mama doesn't want me to. She can't do anything since you left. I mean *nothing*." I take a breath. "You've got to help me."

I have to be Daddy now. I try to think. "Hannah, you already know what to do. I can't help you more than that. I'm dead."

I sag in the chair. "He's still dead," I say. "This is just all pretend."

"It is and it isn't," Caitlin says. "You did just beautifully, Hannah. You really did." She moves to the chair next to me and puts her arm around me. "I like your daddy."

I give a little snort. As if she really met my daddy! "And I like you too."

This time I let her be nice to me.

A couple of days later, I get a letter from Mama. I take it to my room and read it on my bed:

Dear Hannah,

I know they would let me talk to you on the phone, and Rosa said she would be glad to connect us, but you upset me so much during that last call, I just couldn't bear to go through that again. I hope you are feeling better now.

Your therapist, Miss Saunders, came to see me today. She called first, saying that children under psychiatric care are required to have family therapy, but in view of my circumstances, she would be willing to come to the house and talk with me.

She is a pleasant enough looking young woman, but after a few words about you, she started digging into my feelings. Very personal feelings, like how I've felt since Daddy died. She even asked me if I could think of some way that I might have contributed to your breakdown. Me? I told her I didn't see that my feelings had anything to do with what happened to you. I must say I think she came under false pretenses, pretending to be concerned about you but then prying into my private life. They always blame the mother in these situations.

I told her she could come one more time, for your sake, but then, really, I think I'll tell her not to come anymore. I don't like being analyzed like an insect in my own living room. Please cooperate with these people, Hannah, so they won't come around asking me questions. I just can't take it. You know how strangers make me nervous. I love you.

Mama

I crumple the letter and throw it across the room. *She* doesn't like having *her* feelings dug into? *She* doesn't like being analyzed like an insect? *She* doesn't like strangers? What about *me* living with strangers in a strange place and being constantly poked and prodded for every alien feeling? What about *me* imprisoned against my will?

I cross the room and pick up the crunched sheet of paper. "I don't care what you think," I say, and shred her letter into tiny pieces.

Before family therapy, a couple of days later, Poppy paces in our room. She has removed and applied new lipstick three times. Same with the black eye makeup. When she's not fussing with herself, she fusses with me. I let her give me a dark henna rinse that she swears will wash out. We're both beginning to look like spiders. Sting's social worker, Mrs. Homolio, is coming to Poppy's family therapy next hour and she doesn't know why.

"Maybe they'll bring Sting tonight. I only get to see him once a week and it isn't time yet. You want to see him if they bring him? That would be so sweet if they bring him. That kid is so crazy about me. Really. I haven't had anything to drink for six weeks! It's six weeks today! Maybe they think I'm ready to go home. I think I'm almost ready. It's been six weeks." She titters.

"Does your whole family come to therapy?" I ask.

"Just my grandma. She takes care of Sting for me." She checks her teeth for lipstick smudges. There aren't any, but she rubs the two front teeth with an index finger.

Pretty soon it's seven o'clock. "Wish me luck," she says. She crosses herself with crossed fingers and says, "Help me, Buddha, Jesus, Mohammed, and Elohim. Help me." She turns to me. "Sprinkle me with fairy dust," she says.

I sprinkle with both hands and say "Bless, bless."

Calling all gods; calling all gods. Come in, please. Does anyone hear?

In my own family therapy, such as it is, I still find it impossible to talk to Mama. I do talk to Daddy, who tells me he loves me, which is strangely comforting, considering it's coming out of my own mouth. He keeps telling me I already know what to do. Then he says something I don't expect: "Please, Hannah, let me be dead now." I am not so much hurt as lost.

Shortly, after I get back to my room, a high wail comes out of one of the rooms down the hall, and I hear people chattering in low voices, but the wail continues and breaks into gut-wrenching sobs. I stand in the doorway. A nurse leaves the station and hurries down the hall in the direction of the disturbance. "Oh, please, please!" a female voice pleads. Is it Poppy? Then I hear a loud "Sting!" Lots of sobbing. It's hard to listen to. I sit on my bed. Maybe I can do her hair or something when she gets back. She'll feel better soon.

But an hour passes, and Poppy doesn't come back. I sit in the corner of my bed and hug the pregnant Barbie. I try to think of Trilby and me walking home from school, of Bliss behind the counter, of my own bedroom at home with the dried roses hanging from the ceiling. I think of Rosa Benson sitting on her front porch and

Mama hovered over the bonsai. My life. I want my life back. I want to get out of here.

The night nurse comes in and tells me lights will be out in ten minutes. She has brought my pill and some water and stands over me while I drink it down. I get undressed and put on my nightgown. I put Barbie in the drawer next to my bed. The nurse pulls back the cover for me and I get in. "When will Poppy be back?" I ask.

"I'm not sure. She's in the time-out room for a few hours."

"What's wrong? I heard her—"

"She got some upsetting news." She turns off the light.

I just say "Oh," because I know she's not going to tell me more.

She stands over me with her arms folded. "You okay?"

"I guess."

"Good night, then."

Moonlight or just lights from the parking lot light up the room enough for me to see the shadowy posters above Poppy's bed: Sting, the famous, and the Burpee's Oriental Poppy poster. "Oh, baby," I whisper. "Ah, weary wee flipperling." I hum the "Seal Lullaby" to keep my breathing even. It helps. Or maybe it's just the pill.

I don't know how long I've been asleep when Poppy returns. I hear her shuffle about in the half-lit room, hear her get into bed, hear her blowing her nose. "Poppy?"

Silence.

She heaves the grandiflora of sighs. "I'm Rosmarin," she says. "No matter how hard I try, I always end up being just the same old Rosmarin. A loser."

All I can think of is a cheap platitude: No one is a loser who tries. Gag me.

Rosmarin is a pretty name. Better than Poppy. "There's a rose—a miniature—named Rosmarin." I say, "It's pale pink, fragrant, disease resistant, and *very* winter hardy." I look across the room. "That fits you."

Poppy/Rosmarin doesn't even say what a beautiful thought and how she can learn from it, but she doesn't say "screw you" either. Her sniffles come farther apart and finally stop. I lie awake for a while and think about the roses in *Taylor*'s *Guide to Roses* and wish I had the book with me.

The attention in group therapy is focused on Rosmarin the next afternoon. She tells everyone, "Poppy is dead." I expect Caitlin Saunders and the other psychologist, Wes Jenkins, to exchange looks, but they don't. Wes says, "So welcome to group, *Rosmarin*. Want to talk about last night?"

Rosmarin slouches in her chair. "Everybody already knows . . ."

I look around the group to see if this is true, but everyone looks as blank as I feel. Axel even shakes his head.

"I don't think they do know," Wes says.

She chews on a black fingernail and stares at the window beside her. "It doesn't matter," she says.

"Is your baby sick?" Denay, the heavy girl, asks this.

Rosmarin puckers her lips as if she's considering this possibility, but I know she's trying to keep her chin from wobbling. She shakes her head.

It must be her grandmother, I think, but I don't want to draw attention to myself by asking any questions.

We wait.

"Sting," she says, and now her chin does tremble. "They took Sting." Crying. "The county put him in a foster home." Crying. "I'll never get him back."

I'm holding my breath. They can do that? They can just take her baby away?

Lisa asks about Rosmarin's grandmother. "I thought she was taking care of him," she says.

Rosmarin sneers. "She says her arthritis has accelerated, and she can't take care of him anymore. That's the word she used—*accelerated*." Her voice is mimicking. "She says she can't lift him because of the *accelerated* arthritis."

"You don't believe her?" Wes asks.

"Grandma has never used the word *accelerated* in her life! She says, 'Step on it, buster!' That social worker, Mrs. Homolio, told her to say it. She told her to say 'My arthritis has accelerated, Mrs. Homolio hates me. Now she's won." No more crying. Rosmarin's mad.

"She's right about that," Axel says. "Vocabulary is evidence," he says. "It really is. That's how I knew it really wasn't the President who gave the State of the Union message last January . . ." He stops when he sees us staring. "Of course, I wasn't on medication then." He erases his words with a nervous wave of the hand.

Wes says, "Caitlin and I get to decide what's reality."

Stephen, the most intense boy in the group, says, "You're in a power struggle with the social worker."

I tune out as she argues her case. I can't stop swallowing. Could they take my baby away because I'm too young and because Mama can't be of any help? Can they just come in and take her? I mean, how is Mama different than Rosmarin's grandma, whose accelerated arthritis makes her helpless? Mama will be no help in raising my girl—my daughter. "I'd never let anyone take my baby!"

It's when all the voices stop and the faces stare at me that I realize I have spoken aloud. Loud aloud.

"You have a baby too?" Rosmarin asks.

"No, I mean—I'm going to."

Lisa says. "Wowzer. Hannah's pregnant."

"I think it's nice," Denay says. "I'd like to have a baby of my very own."

Stephen grimaces when she says this. "They're not dolls, Denay," he says. "They talk back; they have their own wills."

"I know that," she says, pouting.

"Can we get back to P—uh—Rosmarin?" Wes says. "She's the one who needs our help most immediately."

Yes. Go back to Rosmarin. I hate the attention on me.

"There's nothing now to keep me from being a drunk, now that Sting's gone." Rosmarin sighs.

"Sting didn't keep you from being a drunk before." Stephen's black eyes are intense. "What's the difference?"

Rosmarin's face tightens. "You are such a butthead." Stephen doesn't flinch.

Caitlin gives Stephen a little backup: "I know it sounds harsh . . ." Pause. "But what Stephen said is true. Having Sting hasn't made you stop drinking so far."

"Well, that isn't my fault, is it? Rosmarin whines. "It's that stupid Mrs. Homolio. She'd drive anybody to drink. She hates me."

"Mrs. Homolio doesn't make you drink," Axel says. "She doesn't force it down your throat."

He is sitting right next to Rosmarin and she turns on him, swats him hard on the arm. "What do you know about it? You're the craziest one here. You're—"

"I'm not crazy right now."

Wes says, "No, he's not. I think what Stephen and Axel are trying to say is—"

"That you have to be responsible for your own behavior!" Denay finishes his sentence like it's a catechism. "You drink because you want your problems— your mom, your grandma, your job, Mrs. Homolio, maybe even Sting, all to go away sometimes."

Even though Denay says this gently, Rosmarin is up on her feet, both hands balled into fists. "I have never wanted Sting gone! You're supposed to be supportive!" She blinks tears back. "You can all go to hell!" She stomps out of the room, banging the door shut.

Wes picks up a cellular phone he carries with him and calls the nurses' desk to let them know that Rosmarin is out loose. When he's finished, he says, "Everyone all right?"

Most of the kids nod.

Caitlin looks at me. "Hannah?"

"Will she get him back when she gets out of here? Just because the grandma can't take care of Sting, Rosmarin can. She's his mother." I'm saying too much. I'm showing my hand, but I can't help it. It isn't fair.

"She won't get him back until she can prove she can remain sober over a period of time," Wes says.

My voice sounds too tense when I speak. "Over a period of time? How long? Who gets to decide that? That social worker—Mrs. Homolio—hates Rosmarin. She'll never give Sting back to her." I try to calm my voice, but it is shrill: "Babies belong with their own mothers!"

Denay nods dumbly, but the others stare at me.

Caitlin asks, "Are you talking about Rosmarin or yourself, Hannah?"

Why does she always turn things back on me? "I'm talking about Rosmarin."

"But maybe you're afraid for yourself too," Lisa says quietly.

"You sound pretty defensive," Axel says.

"No, I'm not. I don't think it's fair that the adults get to make all the decisions. Adults aren't always right. There's a lot of nutty adults around. Maybe Mrs. Homolio is one of them. I'm just speaking up for Rosmarin."

Stephen and Lisa exchange a look.

"What?" I say.

Stephen leans forward. "Who are the nutty adults in your life?" he asks.

"That's easy enough," I say without thinking. "My mama is nuttier than a Christmas fruitcake and won't leave the house. My neighbor Mrs. Benson is an obsessive busybody, and the neighbor on the other side, Mrs. Goodrow, thinks she's living in 1935, and Mr. Knight, who has one leg, owns a backhoe in the middle of the city and is digging up our whole neighborhood. And that's just *my* block!"

It's as if I've hit them with a stun gun. Then, to my relief, they break into laughing.

"Gee, is that all?" Wes chides.

"Sounds like you need block therapy," Lisa says.

Their joking relaxes me, and I smile. Caitlin Saunders is looking at the floor.

"We'll pick this up next time," Wes says, looking at his watch. Saved by the clock.

When I return to my bedroom, there's a letter from Mama on my bed. I handle the pink envelope, not sure I want to open it. Finally, I do:

Dear Hannah,

When I told Miss Saunders that I didn't want to see her anymore, she said something so awful, so painful, that I could hardly believe it. She said I could lose you if I didn't make some changes in my life. She said you were making changes, but without my making equally big changes, the two of us wouldn't be able to live together anymore. At first I thought maybe she was threatening me, but she said it in such a calm voice, and there were tears in her eyes as if the thought of us being separated from each other made her sad—"Hannah needs you to be her mother." That's what she said.

Hannah, I don't want to lose you. I will keep seeing Miss Saunders. Do you understand? I will see her twice a week.

Trilby's mother told me they go and see you every Sunday and that you're looking much better, and that you're more cheerful too. That's good, honey. I wish I could see you too. I miss you terribly.

Love, Mama

I read the letter over and over. Mama's in therapy with Caitlin Saunders. I'd like to be a fly on the wall in those sessions.

The next day, when I go into Caitlin's office for private therapy, she has three chairs set up. This can only mean one thing. I have to talk to a chair again. The sun is bright outside the window, but the miniature rosebush has disappeared, I suspect into the waste basket. In its place is a bonsai pine in a clay pot. Did Mama give her that?

Caitlin sees me staring at it. "You must know a little about bonsai?" she says, pointing to a chair.

I sit down. "I know hardly anything about them," I say. "Mama's the expert." I bend my head down so that my hair falls forward and I don't have to see the bonsai or her. "I don't like things in miniature, especially trees," I say. "Trees are meant to be large, free, filling the sky, bending in the wind, not dwarfed by tiny scissors and . . ." I stop. I was going to say tiny minds.

"And?" She sits down next to me.

"Nothing."

"Today I want you to talk to your mother." She sticks that blasted card that says *Mama* on the seat of the chair.

"No." I say. Are Mama and she becoming friends? Are they conspiring against me? That bonsai on the windowsill could be a bribe. "Did Mama give you that bonsai?" I hate myself for asking, but I need to know.

"No, Hannah, I'm taking care of it for one of the psychiatrists who's on vacation."

"Does he know you killed the miniature roses?"

She purses her lips to smother a smile. "He's only going to be gone a week. I think I can manage for that long."

I doubt it. I say, "I don't want to talk to Mama. I have nothing to say to her."

"Is that because you're angry with her?"

"I'm not mad at her."

"You called her 'nutty' last night. That's not exactly a compliment." She runs her fingers down the crease of her pants.

"Well, she is nutty, but that doesn't mean I'm mad." I push my hair behind my ears.

"Let's start there, then. Tell your mama what you think. Tell her she's nutty."

I look at the Mama card. "Oh, for heaven's sake," I say. It's all so stupid.

"Tell her," Caitlin says.

I can tell she's not going to let this go, so I say it. I say, "Mama, I think you're the one who's crazy. I think you belong in here more than I do." Then, without Caitlin's having to tell me, I sit in Mama's chair. She wants to hear Mama? I'll give her Mama. I raise my voice a little. "Oh, Hannah, don't talk that way. That's silly talk. You sound just like your grandma Satterfield. No one ever knew what she was talking about either." I move forward to get up, but Caitlin puts her hand on my knee to hold me back. "Mrs. Ziebarth—Nora," she says, "Hannah thinks you belong here more than she does. Don't you have something to say about that?"

I know what Mama would say to that. "Me? What for? I don't walk around with blood painted on my face. I don't throw someone's precious clay pots over the side of the porch. I don't wave my arms like a tree."

I want to be Hannah now, and I move back to my chair. "But you don't do anything except take care of the bonsai. You don't do *anything*! You don't act like a mother. I want you for once to act like my mother!" My fists come down onto the seat of her chair and knock the cardboard Mama sign over. "I want a mother!" I pound on the sign. "I want a mother! I don't want to be your mother anymore. I want *you* to be the mother." I don't stop pounding the chair, or stop yelling, until I'm too tired to do either. Finally I just lay my head in the chair and whimper: "I want my mother."

Crying makes me feel better for a while after the session, but as I begin thinking of Mama's helplessness, of her missing my junior-high-school graduation, of her insistence that we use cotton place mats and cotton napkins and that they be *ironed,* making extra work for me, the anger builds up all over again, until I find myself in group therapy thrashing on an empty chair with a pillow that Wes keeps conveniently behind his chair. It brings only short-term relief. The anger fumes like black smoke inside me. I think of other kids' parents driving me places because Mama can't. I think of running to the grocery store and making her bag lunches to eat while I'm away, of making dinner and then catching the bus to get to work. I think of her crying for herself when she finds out I'm pregnant.

And I decide I'm not going to live with Mama anymore. I make a budget for myself and the baby to see if we could live on our own. I can make six dollars an hour if I work full-time at the Burger Bar. That's forty hours a week, which comes to two hundred forty dollars a week and nine hundred sixty dollars a month.

There's a newspaper out in the waiting room and I go

out there to look up the apartment ads. One-bedrooms run about five hundred dollars a month. Then food and taxes and baby-sitting. I crumple up the budget sheet. It's not enough. I think about welfare, but it feels sleazy. Everyone knows who's on welfare.

I look through the magazines on the coffee table. You don't really see advertisements unless you have a direct interest in the product or the method of selling. Like now I notice all ads with babies in them, when I never even saw them before. A decorating magazine has an ad for Martex sheets, "soft and cozy sheets for adults," but the ad shows two babies half covered in white bedding. I can't take my eyes off those babies, about a year old, laughing and showing tiny scalloped teeth.

In a fashion magazine, I see an ad for Little Me baby wear with a large close-up of a baby, smiling; its eyes shiny half-moons, a tiny nose and lips curving up, one hand reaching out in soft focus. The baby hair is light, wavy wisps sweeping smoothly out from its perfect head. I look to see if anyone sees me and carefully tear the ad from the magazine.

I hang her—she's wearing a pink quilted top with lavender trim—above my bed. Baby. Sweet baby of mine. How can I make a life for us?

I want to talk to someone outside the hospital. I decide to call Trilby. I've been a model patient for weeks, reaching and staying at level three. Level three is not the highest level, which is four, but no one wants to be at kiss-up level four. Level threes can make outgoing calls, although one of the nurses has to stand by and listen to everything you say to make sure you're not making any drug deals or *engaging in any inappropriate behavior,* a phrase that all the therapists love to throw around. I ask Nancy if I can make a phone call.

"Are you calling a family member?" she asks me.

"I can't talk to my mother. We upset each other." The truth makes me sad. "I just want to talk to my friend, Trilby."

"Go ahead," she says.

I dial out of habit. "Hello," a male voice says. A familiar male voice. "Hello?" It is Milo. I have dialed Milo by mistake. "Anybody there?" Pause. Pause. Pause. He hangs up. I stand with the phone against my ear, listening to the dial tone. Finally I say to Nancy, "There's nobody home."

So how are you, Milo? Are you noticing babies everywhere you look? Michelin babies, Martex babies, Gerber babies? Do you look in the mirror and think about our baby looking like you, playing soccer, swimming with water wings in your parents' pool? Do you ever think about me? Do you ever miss me?

I wander to the window at the end of the nurses' station and look out. Steam is rising from the asphalt parking lot, reminding me it's summer—a good season for miracles.

Rosmarin notices the baby picture I cut out of the magazine when she returns from her own therapy. "I guess you're keeping your baby," she says, standing in front of my bed.

"Yes," I say.

"They'll try and talk you out of it, you know."

"Who?"

"Every adult who crosses your path." She turns away and lies on her own bed. "You're too young to care for a baby—that's what they'll say." She stares at the ceiling.

"I'll be sixteen when I have it."

Rosmarin snorts. "A regular old lady," she says. "Does your mother think you should keep it?"

I think of Mama saying I should give the baby up for adoption.

"What about the baby's old man? Does he want you to keep it?"

I can't speak the answers to these questions.

"I thought not," Rosmarin says.

"*I* want to keep it. That's what's important. I'm its mother."

Rosmarin turns and faces the wall. "Keep hanging baby pictures on your wall," she says. "Maybe you can fight off the adult propaganda. Maybe you can wish yourself a happy ending."

I want to know what she means by adult propaganda, but not as much as I want her to shut up, so I don't say anything. At least I'm not a drunk, I think. But it is little comfort.

When I have been in the hospital a month, I am allowed to go on an outing without the group and the therapists. Trilby, who just passed her driver's test, invites me to an outdoor concert at the Gallivan Center, which is the park right downtown with an open-air bowl and a reflecting pool that becomes an ice rink in winter.

"Is it a rock concert?" Caitlin asks me when I ask permission to go. We are in her office and the bonsai pine has been replaced with a new philodendron, a perfect plant for her. It's unkillable.

"I don't think so. It's part of a regular Thursday series. I think it's ethnic music or something."

"That's fine, but there are some rules I want you to follow." She raises her eyebrows slightly as if she's waiting for a rebellion, but I am chemically smooth and cool.

I nod, waiting.

"I don't want you to see your mother, so don't drop by your house. Okay?"

"I won't," I say. Easy. I don't want to see Mama, period.

"And you have to be back by ten-thirty."

I salute her and she smiles and waves me off. "Have fun," she says.

At first I feel nervous being in the car with Trilby. I don't know if it's the awkwardness of being with her again or just her driving, which is terrifying.

"Can you believe I'm actually driving?" Trilby looks at me when she talks and the car swerves a little. "Oops," she says, overcorrecting; we're all over the road. "I can't talk and drive at the same time."

Geez, no kidding.

"My dad said he would buy me a used car when I go

to college." She nudges my arm and the car swerves to the right. "We can drive down to Cedar City together. Won't that be a kick?"

We were on the Cedar City campus last summer for a church youth conference and made a pact late at night in the dorm that we would return together for college as roommates. A lifetime ago—that pact.

"I don't know if I'll be going to college," I say.

"Oh my gosh!" One hand covers her mouth. The car jolts around a curve. "I completely forgot. I'm so stupid!"

"It's okay," I say. "Watch the road." I laugh nervously.

"I can't talk and drive at the same time," she says again.

We're speeding along 11th Avenue, above the cemetery, toward City Creek, and pretty soon we'll be at the spot where Milo and I did it the first time, and where I got pregnant. "Let me do the talking then," I say, but all I can think of is Milo and me in the backseat of the 4Runner.

Trilby giggles. "Well, talk, then."

We're there. By the mausoleum. "That's where I got pregnant," I say, pointing to a little turnoff.

The car lurches to the left. An oncoming car honks. "Ayyyy," Trilby squeals, "I didn't want to know that!" She steadies the wheel with both hands. At the stop sign on I Street, she waits too long and then pulls out as a car approaches. He has to brake for her. "Sorry!" she cries, waving to the guy, who points at his forehead.

"This is not a restful drive for a mental patient," I say.

She breaks up laughing. "And you thought you had *real* problems," she says.

I laugh with her. This is just Trilby, my oldest friend. If she doesn't kill me, I can relax.

From City Creek, we drive downtown and into the American Stores parking terrace across the block from the Gallivan Center. Trilby has promised me dinner, and I ask if we can go to the Burger Bar so I can thank Bliss, my boss, for the candy she sent me.

Bliss and Dennis are behind the counter. Dennis blushes when he sees me and nods a "hi," but Bliss yells in her smoker's voice, "Hey, you're looking a lot better than the last time I saw you." She inspects the scar over my one eye. "At least there's no blood! It's just yellow and green here." Then she sees the smaller scar and bruise on the other eye. "Hey, did he hit you twice?" She doesn't wait for an answer. "What a slime pit. I hope you sued his socks off."

"I'm thinking about it," I say, although the thought is totally new to me—I don't know where it came from.

Trilby, looking startled, says, "Really?"

I shrug quickly and thank Bliss for the chocolates. "It's the first box of chocolates I've ever had to myself," I say.

Bliss nods, embarrassed to be considered a nice person. She turns to Dennis. "Two Burger Bar Specials on the house," she says. She brings out two trays and fills two large cups with chocolate shake. "Guess what?"

she says. "I'm going to be the day manager starting September."

"Cool," I say. "Will you have work for me? I mean full-time?" In my peripheral vision, I see Trilby's jaw drop.

"Want a fast-food career?" Bliss assembles our order as Dennis brings her each item. "It's a smart choice. Fast food is the American way."

I see in her face that she actually believes this, and it depresses me. I mean she sounds like she's selling flags or something. Suddenly I'm hyperaware how shabby and greasy the place is, how unflattering the uniform, the bright orange trim against the brown polyester, and how the opaque glass light dishes hanging from the ceiling are filled with dead flies.

"We're always short on help these days. Not many people see the opportunities in a fast-food career. I'd be a maniac not to take you on."

It's nice to hear that somebody thinks I'm good at something, and I smile. "Thanks," I say.

Trilby waits until we are seated at a table and I have unwrapped my Bravo Burger. "You're not quitting high school, are you?" She whispers so she won't offend Bliss in case *she* hasn't finished, which I know she has, but just barely. Bliss once told me that you weren't a grown-up down in Sanpete County until you'd stolen a car. It was more important to commit a felony than to finish high school.

"I may have to quit," I tell Trilby.

"You can't!" Her voice squeaks. She's not a naturally

confrontive person, which is why we get along. "You just can't—high school is minimal. You can't do a thing without it."

My mouth is full of Bravo Burger; still, I manage to garble out: "I have a baby to raise. I need money."

Trilby, who hasn't even unwrapped her hamburger, looks stricken, as if I just told her I was having a full-body tattoo. "You're keeping it? You're keeping the baby?"

She makes me feel defensive, and my voice sounds harsh when I speak: "Yes, I'm keeping it. I'm its mother." I sound like Poppy—Rosmarin.

"How can you? I mean, you're not old enough!" A splotchy red rash runs up her neck and onto her cheeks.

She's pissing me off with her prim ways. "Wouldn't you keep your baby if you were pregnant?" I ask a little too loudly.

Trilby's blotched skin turns florid, and she glances nervously at the man wearing a baseball cap eating at the table next to us. "Me?" The idea is completely foreign. "I don't think I could. I'm not ready." She looks into her lap. "I'd have to give it up for adoption."

What a little coward, I think, but I say, "That's just adult propaganda." I'm quoting Rosmarin. "It's irresponsible."

"No." She shakes her head and looks directly at me. "I think it's irresponsible not to." Her voice softens. "I couldn't do it alone, and that means my parents would have to help raise it. It wouldn't be fair to them."

As much as I wanted to leave the hospital, I now

want to go back. Before I can say anything, Bliss heads toward our table, waving an envelope. She sets it down in front of me. "This is your last paycheck. I wasn't sure when you'd be back. I almost sent it to your mother, but—"

"Oh, thanks," I say, relieved to be free of Trilby, at least for a few seconds.

"What are you guys doing tonight?" Bliss asks.

"We're going to the concert at the Gallivan Center," I say.

"Music for a Gloomy World," Trilby says.

I haven't heard this before. "Huh?" I turn to her.

She nods. It's so apt. Trilby seems to realize it at the same time and we break into laughing.

Bliss squints at us. "Guess I missed something." She turns away. "Anyway," she says, walking back to the counter, "call me when you get out of the asylum." She lets out this big snort. About a half dozen customers turn to stare. "I'll be your fast-food mentor."

Fast-food mentor extraordinaire.

Trilby sips her Salivating Shake and looks up. "Hannah," she says. "I should mind my own business. I'm sorry."

I wave off her apology. "It's okay. I was being defensive."

She's biting her lip, looking miserable.

"Really," I say. "I think I need some music for a gloomy world."

She smiles then. We eat quickly and call good-bye to Bliss, who's on the phone, her back toward us, a finger in one ear. There's a big grease stain on her butt.

There must be a couple of thousand people at the Gallivan Center, sitting on the grass at the edge of the reflecting pool, on cement planters or gliding on Rollerblades around the periphery. Some people have brought lawn chairs from home, some have picnics, and a lot of them have babies. Babies in strollers. Babies on hips. The guy standing next to us is wearing hospital greens and a beeper. He holds a baby on his shoulders. He yells when the baby pulls his hair as hard as he can or tries to bite his head. "Hey, Frodo," the guy calls up, laughing. "Give me a break already."

The mother tries to dislodge Frodo's fingers from his dad's hair, but he hangs on tight. Then she sings "Patty Cake," and the baby lets go to clap along with his mother.

When they're finished, the baby looks at me, and I make faces. He flaps his fat arms in the air and giggles.

Trilby grins.

"How could you give a baby like *that* up?" I snap at her.

It's like I've slapped her. Her face wobbles. "I'm not stupid, Hannah—I know it's not easy." She presses her lips tightly to gain control of her emotions. "But you're not the only one suffering in the world." She's barely finished when the band starts up with a rhythmic, loud number from old Mexico. The crowd cheers and claps along. Trilby's lips form a tight line and she keeps her head averted, clapping listlessly behind the beat.

What is it with me? Am I only fit company for paid therapists? Why do I sound like I'm always picking a fight? The next number is louder and faster and obvious dance music; the people in the lawn chairs are up on their feet, dancing with each other. The man and woman and baby dance in circles, laughing. On the other side of Trilby, two guys, wearing identical tank tops, flail their arms and bump hips on the strong beats. Music for a Gloomy World, a band made to order for us: I'm standing with my hands in my pockets, feeling lumpy, while Trilby claps out of rhythm, looking anywhere but my way.

When the music stops and the cheering dies down, Trilby says, "I'm going to go sit on that bench over there." She points across the reflecting pool. She is still hurt.

"You can't see the band from there," I say.

"I don't care. I've got to sit for a while. I'll be back in a few minutes." She doesn't invite me along, and I turn and watch her walk away, wondering if I should follow. Am I supposed to be by myself away from the hospital? Is there a rule in the orientation booklet for this occasion?

The band saves me from my indecision. They play something my daddy used to sing with the guitar. I sing the words, "When it's springtime in the Rockies . . ." The sky is now a deep lilac and the city trees stand like parrot cages draped in darkness for sleep. I look up and take a deep breath. I'm outside. I'm okay. When Trilby comes back, I will apologize. I will be a better guest.

Next, they play the "Hokey Pokey," which I haven't heard since grade school. Everyone is up on their feet putting their left foot in, their left foot out, their left foot in and shaking it about. I sing louder now, and the baby, Frodo, who is now being held by his mother, turns when he hears my voice. I shake my hands in front of his face and he buries his head in her shoulder. I will do the "Hokey Pokey" with my baby. Hokey Pokey; that's what it's all about!

I'm putting my backside in, my backside out, when Trilby returns, breathless. She couldn't have sat for more than a couple of minutes. She grabs my arm with both hands. "Did you see him?" she asks wide-eyed.

"Who?" I ask, waving my free arm.

"You didn't see him?" She has to yell to be heard over the crowd's singing. "He was walking this way."

I shake my head, wondering what movie star is in town.

She speaks his name at the same time I see his face about twenty feet away, tan, handsome, handsomer than I remember. He's wearing the matching shirt to the one hidden in my suitcase in the hospital. The U.S. Soccer Association shirt.

"Milo's here!" Trilby says.

"Milo." I can't take my eyes off him.

Trilby glances back. "Do you want to go?" She's already shoving me in the opposite direction.

"No, I mean . . ." Shouldn't I be angry? I want to watch Milo do the Hokey Pokey. His body is elegant, I think. "Wait a minute," I say.

"What a colossal creep!" Trilby is incensed for me, who cannot be angry at something so beautiful. If I had told him differently, on the porch swing, with lemonade—if I hadn't acted so needy.

Mimi comes up behind him and hands him one of two ice cream cones. They're both chocolate. Does she know that Milo's favorite flavor is pistachio?

When Trilby sees her, she says, "I should have known."

Mimi dances lightly on her toes in front of Milo. He kisses her shoulder and she pulls her long hair to the side so he can kiss her neck.

Trilby studies my face. "I think we should go," she says.

"I guess," I say.

Mimi sees me first and whispers to Milo. Trilby is pulling me through the crowd, but I can't look away. The last thing I see before turning my head is Milo's sneer and his fist raised, middle finger up.

Crossing the street to the parking lot, we can hear the "Bunny Hop," and the crowd shouting, "Hop, hop, hop." Long, snaking lines of people hop forward. I try to look for the baby and his parents, but they are lost in the crowd. Milo hates me. That cruel gesture—he hates me. I cannot seem to hate back. I just feel shabby. Ashamed. I'll probably have to speak to him as a chair for the rest of my life: Milo you hurt me. Blah, blah, blah. Boring, boring, boring. I am too boring to love.

"Are you all right?" Trilby asks me when we are seated in her car. Her hand touches my knee. "Hannah?"

I realize I'm sitting the way I do in Caitlin's office

sometimes, hugging myself, my head forward with hair falling down over my face. Caitlin calls it my "cave position." I'm hiding behind my hair. I look up. "I'm fine," I say. "I have to go back to the hospital now." More than anything I want to rock back and forth in the seat and hum. Rock, rock. But I can't do that in front of Trilby. I would feel so much better if I could just rock. "Please, I have to go back," I say.

"Okay," she says.

The drive to the hospital is a blur. I look into my lap, where I can see Milo's sneer and his finger raised, and I hold myself tight and try not to feel anything. A deep hum from the back of my throat could drown out everything. In a minute I'll be back in the hospital. Safe. Safe to hum and rock.

"We're here," Trilby says.

"I'm sorry." Sorry for scaring her with my life's plans. Sorry for being mental. "Thank you."

"I wasn't a very good listener," she says.

"My fault." I open the car door. My body feels so heavy.

"Listen," she says. "When you have your baby, will you let me baby-sit sometimes? I'm a really good baby-sitter."

Knowing that Trilby doesn't think I should keep the baby at all, this offer of help is more kindness than I can take in at this moment. I nod my head and try to smile and then walk up the hospital steps.

She yells good-bye. I wave without turning.

I check in at the desk in front of the adolescent unit

and the nurse buzzes me in. I'm home. The night nurse wheels the medications on a cart. I take mine in the hall. I'm relieved that Rosmarin is not in the room. I don't turn on the lights. I kick off my shoes and get into bed, sit against the wall with the blankets up over my shoulder, hug myself, and begin to rock and hum. Rock, rock. Rock Milo and his obscene gesture away. He really is not coming to save me. I had hoped. Foolish, foolish girl. He really hates me. He hates *us*. Baby and me. I cry. I rock. I hum.

In the morning, I don't get up. I am too heavy to walk. The nurse—is it Nancy or Jeannette?—cajoles me. I'm doing so well, she says. I'll drop a level if I stay in bed.

I am too heavy for level three. Let me drop. I'll drop. I spend time in the isolation room in a thick sleep.

It is Caitlin Saunders who comes to get me. I don't know if it's morning or afternoon. I follow her to her office. The asphalt parking lot outside a window I pass shimmers with a wobbly heat. It is summer, that's all I know.

When we are seated in her office, Caitlin asks, "What happened when you were out last night?"

My head droops, face hidden behind my hair. I don't want to think about this.

She lifts my chin with her hand. I can't avoid her eyes. "Hannah?"

My face crumbles and I cry, telling her about seeing Milo and Mimi between shudders, describing what he did. "He hates me. It's my fault." I cover my face with my hands and wail.

Caitlin moves her chair forward so that our knees are touching and holds my arm. When I've cried myself out, she says, "Tell me about the father of your baby." It is the first time she has asked about Milo directly. I figure that before this she thought I wasn't ready to talk about him.

"Milo Fabiano." I spell his last name for her. "It's Italian," I say.

She smiles and waits.

I look down at my hands. My nails look scuzzy and I bite at a ragged edge. Fleeting images of Milo fast-forward through my head: Milo playing soccer; Milo's mouth in a half smile. The curve of his bare backside. Milo's fist. My hair covers my face like a veil, and I push a large section behind my ear and see the sky glimmer blue beyond the wired window. "I don't remember . . ." I say. And it's true. I can't focus on any memory before last night long enough to form a sentence about him.

"How did you meet him?" Caitlin's voice is light, soft, as if this is no big deal, as if we're talking about the weather: when did you first notice it was raining?

"At a soccer game last February." I fill in briefly about being hit in the nose with the ball and Milo taking me home. "I couldn't believe that somebody that handsome would even talk to me."

She waits for me to tell more. She sits forward in her chair, one elbow resting on her knee, her hand holding her chin, the other hand rubbing my knee. "Tell me," she says.

I look away from her briefly, twisting my hair with

my fingers, and when I look back her face still stares into mine, her eyebrows raised, waiting. "Tell, Hannah. It will help. Tell all of it," she whispers.

I grasp her hand and rock back and forth in my chair. "We had been dating more than a month," I say, and then I tell it the way I always tell it:

Milo wasn't the first boy to kiss me but he was the first to bite me. I said "Ouch" and he said, "Let me lick it better." It was when his mouth was on my shoulder and his hands tugged my camisole down that I knew I would go all the way with him. I would lose my virginity with Milo in the back of his Toyota 4Runner parked above the cemetery with the lights of Salt Lake City below. Not that we were looking. I kissed him fiercely. Too fiercely. He said, "Slow down; it's better slow." I didn't want slow. I pulled him down on me. "Now," I said. "Now."

It was when Milo was in me that the announcer on the television said, "The Mailman delivers," and Milo arched his torso back and yelled, "The Mailman delivers. The Mailman delivers!"

I stop.

Caitlin shifts in her chair. "There was a television?"

"Yes. He has this tiny portable that plugs into the cigarette lighter. Milo can't stand to miss a Jazz game and they were playing the Lakers that night."

"Where was the television?"

This seems like an odd question, but I answer it: "It was propped against the back of the bucket seat. The cord was long enough so that he could pull it into the back with us."

She nods. " 'The Mailman delivers' means that—"

"Karl Malone scored. That's what that Hot Rod Hundley guy—the announcer for the Jazz—always says when Karl Malone scores. He says, 'And the Mailman delivers.' "

Her head tilts slightly as if she doesn't get it. "So when Milo yelled—you did say he yelled?—"

"Yes."

"—when he 'yelled' he was happy because?"

"Because Karl Malone scored!" Could she be more dense?

"And?"

I look away then and think of Milo's urgent rocking, his chest arched away, his attention focused on the television, his one hand turning up the sound so that the roar of the crowd filled the car and above that his yelling, "The Mailman delivers." When I look back at Caitlin Saunders her face is as sad as I feel. "I think Milo was happy because he and Karl Malone scored at the same time," I say.

She nods again. "I think so too," she says.

We sit and look at each other. For the first time, I see that her eyes brim with tears.

"You want to know something funny?" I say after a little while.

"What?"

"The Jazz lost."

Back in my room, I notice that Rosmarin's posters are gone. In fact, when I look in her closet and the desk drawers, all her stuff is gone. Was it gone last night and

I was too out of it to notice? Her bed looks too neat, and when I check, there is no bedding, just a bedspread pulled over a bare mattress and pillow.

At the nurses' station, I ask Nancy where Rosmarin went.

"Her grandmother came to get her last night—said the insurance ran out."

"She's gone home?"

Nancy nods and smiles. "It does happen, although usually not quite so abruptly."

"She didn't say good-bye."

"Well, she did in her own way," Nancy says. "She said 'Good riddance' on her way out."

I smirk. It sounds just like Rosmarin.

Later, when I'm filling out a study sheet on *The Scarlet Letter,* I find a bottle of black nail polish in my desk drawer with a note around it: "Hey, Hannah, don't let the adults get to you. It's our world too. Call me sometime. I got some maternity clothes you can borrow. See ya, Ros." Already she is reinventing herself with a shortened version of her name. She's written in her phone number. I try to imagine what Rosmarin's maternity clothes might look like. Neo-gothic, no doubt. I slip the note into my binder. I will call her later. Then I paint my nails black in memory of Poppy-Rosmarin-Ros.

I try to keep a low profile in group therapy. Rosmarin's advice about volunteering to speak on things you don't much care about works surprisingly well, but the next afternoon Caitlin says, "Why don't you take a little time today, Hannah."

I'm slouched into a stuffed chair, my leg dangling over the arm; I'm expecting someone to volunteer, which is what usually happens. Someone has an "issue" they want to bring to the group. Or someone just wants to be told they're okay. I know Denay wants to talk, because she says so before we even sit down.

"Uh . . ." I pull my leg from the arm of the chair and sit up. "Sure." I swallow hard. "I thought Denay was going first." I can't think of anything to say. They already know I'm pregnant.

"Did your parents freak about your pregnancy?" Brenda asks.

"Mama freaked." I rub my hand across the scratchy orange fabric along the arm of my chair. Institutional fabric, Mama would call it. I can't control a nervous giggle. "My dad died two years ago—he had a respiratory failure." They don't need to know about the burp. Respiratory failure is close enough.

"Did she knock you around when she found out?" This comes from Lisa, who has been knocked around a lot by both of her parents.

"No—my mother wouldn't—no." I press the wound over my eye. The stitches are dissolving. "It was my boyfriend. When I told him I was pregnant, he hit me . . ." I feel outside my body, drifting and floating about the room, watching and hearing myself talk. Who is this strange girl with this strange story? "I thought he would marry me, but he hit me," I say.

Milo wasn't the first boy to kiss me, but he was the first one to bite me.

Lisa bites her bottom lip. "How many times did he hit you?" she asks.

I don't think carefully. I say, "Once."

I think I have forgotten something, but what could it be? It occurs to me that I will go to hell for forgetting. How strange that I, who thinks there cannot possibly be a God after what's happened to me and my family— that I still believe in hell.

All of this takes the few milliseconds between my answer and the question Stephen raises. The question I have not wanted to think about: "Where did the other cut come from?" Stephen asks.

Not right now. Let me tell my story first. "My mother is one of those people who won't leave the house because she's so afraid. She's been that way since my father died."

"Agoraphobia," Axel tells the others. He knows about every mental illness known to man.

I nod. "Yes, that's it. She had to have our neighbor bring the papers to her to sign me in here. She won't even come out on the front porch. She can't touch the screen door!" I distract them successfully for several minutes with my mother's illness. I tell them about the bonsai plants, how she's one of the most knowledgeable people in the state about bonsai. How people come to see some of her plants because they're so exotic.

"You and your mom are kind of alike with your interests in plants—" Brenda says.

"No!" It comes out too loud. I soften it. "No," I say more softly. "I don't like bonsai. I hate miniature trees. Trees should be full grown. They should create shade—"

"I mean your interest in roses. You love roses and know everything about them, and she loves her bonsai plants. That's a little the same, don't you think?" Brenda's voice shrinks to a tiny volume. My loud "no" scared her.

"I don't really think so." But my words have an angry edge to them that I don't intend. *Madness runs in families.*

Stephen repeats his question: "Where did the other cut come from?"

The trouble with suicidal people like Stephen is that they have nothing to lose. They can say anything they want, no matter how much it might hurt a person. He's the one who said to Rosmarin that Sting had never kept her from drinking before. It was cruel. It was why she got so mad that day and walked out. Why don't the therapists stop Stephen? Can't they see what he's doing?

"What?" I ask.

"How did you get the smaller cut on the left eye? You have stitches beside your left eye too. He couldn't have cut both eyes with one punch."

"Maybe he hit me twice." One blow is so asymmetrical. That's what I thought that night in front of the mirror, the night I now do not want to remember. I did something.

"What a creep," Lisa says.

"Boys generally are—" Denay says.

"Hey!" Link Bailey says. "Not all pigeons are flying rats!"

Denay giggles. "Present company excepted . . ."

Everyone is smiling. Even Lisa smiles behind the biting lips. Not Stephen, though. He looks hard at me. "I think you should think about how many times he hit you," he says. "I mean, you said 'once' as if it were a sure thing—"

"He beat her up, okay?" Denay says. "What does it matter how many times he hit her?"

I look to Caitlin, who looks from me to Stephen and back again. Wes watches Stephen.

"You guys are the therapists." I turn to them. "Does it matter how many times he hit me? I have two cuts. He must have hit me twice, then."

Caitlin turns to Lisa. "What do you think, Lisa?"

Lisa leans forward, her elbows on her knees—she rubs her face with both hands as if she's trying to wipe something away. She shakes her head back and forth like she doesn't want to speak. Then she sits back in her chair, lifts her T-shirt high enough so that we can see the edge of her bra. Her abdomen is covered with scars. Some long, some short. Some are smooth lines, some are jagged. At least a dozen of them. Maybe more. She unbuttons her jeans to show more scars around her waist. "Razor cuts," she says evenly. "I did them myself."

"Oh," I say, my mouth twisted in a little oval. "Oh,

oh, oh." Lisa's scars remind me. I rock back and forth. "Oh, oh, oh. He hit me once—here. Milo hit me here. I fell against the Dumpster and knocked my head. He said I was a whore." Rock, rock. "I went to his house—oh, oh, oh. He was with Mimi—oh—I hid in the back of the 4Runner. They made out. Oh, oh, oh. I remember being a tree and swaying my branches. I remember being a wild thing and painting my face with blood. I made more blood with Daddy's old razor blade. I'm bad. Oh, oh, oh."

The whole hour is spent on me, although I don't always feel present in the room. I do remember Lisa saying, "You felt you deserved it."

"Most of us are here because we deserve punishment." Stephen says that. I remember, because he doesn't say, "We *think* we deserve it," he says, "We deserve punishment." Poor Stephen. Wes corrects him, but Stephen, always grim looking, I can tell, doesn't believe him.

After the others leave, Caitlin stays and asks me if I've ever cut myself before. I tell her no, and that's true.

"I needed to be here—in the hospital—didn't I?" I ask her.

"Yes, you did."

"Will I get better?"

"Yes. You've already come a long way."

While I'm eating ninety percent of my dinner—everything but the canned peas—my statement echoes around in my head: "I needed to be in the hospital." The funny thing about the peas, which are truly disgusting, is that Brenda, the one with multiple eating disorders, eats *only* the peas. No one else can stomach them, and Brenda eats every last one on her plate. She doesn't touch the Salisbury steak or the mashed potatoes or the apple juice or the chocolate pudding with Cool Whip. I see that and know that I needed to be hospitalized just as much as Brenda. We're both Looney Tunes. Just in different ways. *Looney Tunes* isn't a proper psychological term but I think it's pretty accurate.

I have chocolate pudding in my mouth when it hits me: If I was wrong about needing to be hospitalized, then I could have been wrong about other things and *people* as well. I have to make a phone call. Jeanette, the night nurse, is on duty at the desk and I ask her if I can make a phone call.

"Sure." She doesn't even ask who I'm calling, which is *real* inappropriate behavior for a nurse in this unit.

"I need to use the phone directory."

She pulls the directory out of a drawer and hands it to me. I look up the number, take a "cleansing breath"—another phrase I learned in the hospital—and dial.

The phone rings at least a half dozen times and I think maybe she's not home and don't know whether I'm relieved or disappointed, but then I hear Rosa Benson's strong voice say hello.

I don't know what to call her, so I go for the polite. "Mrs. Benson?"

"Yes." Her voice is impatient, like she thinks I'm a telemarketer.

"This is Hannah. Hannah Ziebarth."

Dumbfounded pause. Like I've just pulled all her rosebushes out by the roots. "Hannah!" Her voice softens. "Your mother didn't tell me you were coming home."

"I'm not home. I'm calling from the hospital."

Jeanette, the nurse, looks over her glasses at me.

I turn my back on her and lower my voice. "I'm calling to—you know—apologize for stealing your roses and—uh—and for the way I behaved that night—you know—before I came to the hospital . . ."

Second dumbfounded pause.

"And," I continue, "I want to thank you for helping Mama sign me in to the hospital. I didn't know it at the time, but I really needed help." *You can't believe how much help.*

"You know, Hannah"—Rosa Benson finds her voice—"as irritating as it was for me to have you stealing my roses, I've missed our sparring. It's downright boring in the mornings when you're away."

I give way to a giddy snicker. "That's nice of you to say, but I know I was a pain in the neck."

"Okay," she says. "You were a bit of a pain." She laughs. "I can be a pain myself. We're alike that way."

Boy, I can hardly believe it. I'm having a real civilized conversation with Rosa Benson and she's actually nice.

"How are you feeling?" she asks.

"A lot better," I say. "Sometimes I still get really

angry, but it helps to talk about it." I don't say how I can't even think about Mama without exploding and I can't think of Milo without imploding. Either way, I'm an angry mess sometimes.

"Yes, talking does help. I had therapy when I got very depressed after my husband died. It saved my life. Maybe literally." She's sharing personal stuff with me like I'm an adult. "How about physically? Is the pregnancy making you ill?"

"No, I feel strong, actually. Some smells—eggs and canned peas—make me a little nauseous, but I haven't thrown up or anything."

"Must be all that wonderful estrogen." Her voice sounds wistful.

"Yeah." I can't think of more to talk about. "Well, I just wanted to tell you—you know—that I know I was a jerk—"

"You're a very responsible young woman, Hannah." She's dead serious. "I should apologize to you for not recognizing it sooner and for not helping more after your father died."

Now *I'm* dumbfounded. "No, no. It's not necessary."

"I know now what you've taken on in the last two years and it's much more than any young girl should have to do. I'm sorry I didn't see it sooner." She takes a breath. "I'm really sorry."

I don't know what to say. "It's—It's—okay—really," I stammer.

"Will you let me come and get you when you're ready to be released?"

"I don't know when that will be—"

"I'll be here."

"Okay."

"You'll let me know?"

"Yes."

"Thanks for calling, Hannah. It means a lot to me."

"Uh—okay."

"Get well."

"I will. Bye."

"Good-bye, dear."

Rosa Benson called me dear. *Dear.* She apologized to me the same way the bishop did. I feel good.

I put the phone down and thank Jeanette, who smiles at me as if I've just passed the personal phone call test with honors.

That night, just after the lights are out and I'm lying in bed, I feel a little flutter deep inside me. I'm just imagining, I think. But the flutter continues rhythmically, and I know it's my baby. I lay my hand on my abdomen and feel a tiny ripple of movement. Magic. Ah, weary wee flipperling, curl at thy ease.

For the first time in many weeks, I have this feeling that I can't put a name to. It's not anything as manic as happiness but it's a feeling of well-being, of health. I tell Caitlin this at our next session in her office.

She nods thoughtfully. "Why do you think you feel so good?" she asks.

"Can't I just feel better without having to analyze?" I think it's a crummy question.

"Humor me," she says.

"Well, the talk with Rosa Benson made me feel good . . ." I don't tell her about the baby fluttering inside me. That's my own secret.

"You don't think Mrs. Benson is out to get you anymore?"

"Hardly." I grin. "It was more like I was out to get *her*. I was wrong about her."

She nods that all-knowing nod with the all-knowing smile. "Have you been wrong before about people?" She moves forward in her seat, one elbow resting on the arm of her chair, her hand underneath her chin.

"Well, Milo, obviously." Can't we spend one hour just talking like friends? Does it always have to be therapy? I feel some of my energy draining away. "I didn't have a clue about Milo."

She nods. "Anyone else?"

I can't think of anyone. "No," I say.

She doesn't move or take her eyes off me. She waits for my answer, only I don't have an answer. Am I supposed to guess what's on her mind?

Finally she says, "What about your mother?"

"Mama?" What is she talking about? I look out the window and try to remember. "What was the question?" I ask. I look into my lap.

"Is it possible that you've misjudged your mother?"

My head shoots up. "You're kidding, aren't you? I *live* with my mother. I know what she's like. She's crazy. Are you trying to make me say she isn't crazy? Are you? Are you trying to make me say I'm crazy and she's not? Is that what you want me to say? Because you can forget it." Any good feeling I had coming into Caitlin's office is now gone. I press my lips together tightly. I won't look at her.

"I don't think you're crazy, Hannah." She thinks for a second. "Let me ask you in a different way: Did you think your mother was crazy before your dad died?"

"I don't remember—"

"Don't be so quick—take a minute to think. How old were you?"

"Thirteen, going on fourteen."

"What grade were you in?"

"Eighth. Actually I missed the last week of school because he died. I missed graduation from middle school."

"Do you remember telling me that your mother missed your middle-school graduation as evidence that she didn't support you?" She sits back and folds her hands in her lap. "I'm wondering if you've confused other facts about your mother. Is it possible that the last two years with her, which I admit have been unusually hard, have colored your memory of the first thirteen-plus years of your life with her?"

"Why are we talking about Mama? I don't want to talk about her." I stand up. The room is suffocating. "Why should I worry about her? Has she worried about me? Has she even once asked how I was doing? Has she? I'm not talking about her anymore." I swing around to leave.

"Sit down, Hannah." Caitlin's voice is forceful and authoritative.

I stop short of the door.

"Sit down," she says again.

I sit, my jaw locked tightly. I think I'm getting a headache.

Caitlin's voice is softer. "I'll ask you the same question you just asked—have you once during your stay here asked about how your mother is doing? I have been seeing her as long as I've seen you. Aren't you curious?"

I think about her question. She's right. I haven't asked. "No," I say. "Frankly, I don't care how she's doing."

She sighs. "You sound the same way you used to sound when you talked about Rosa Benson."

"It's not the same."

"I want you to think about your relationship with your mother before your dad died. It's an assignment. I want you to write down any memories you have in your journal. And I want to see it the next time we meet. Do you understand?"

I won't look at her, but I nod yes. Yes, Mistress of the Psyche. Yes, ma'am. Yes, Queen of the Night. Yes, Your Royal Highness.

"Tomorrow night, your uncle Sewell is coming to meet with you for family therapy."

"Sewell Satterfield!" I can't help looking at her now. She's thrown me a lulu. "Why? He barely knows anything about our family. He just owns the Burger Bar where I work."

"He's your uncle, and he knows more than you think."

"He knows diddly squat."

"Remember you said that your mother always says you're like your grandma Satterfield?"

I nod.

"Well, Sewell was her son. He can tell us about her."

"She was crazy."

"That's your mother talking. Maybe your mother and Sewell see their own mother in different ways."

"Crazy is crazy," I say.

"Aren't you curious?"

I shrug and make a face. I can't imagine having an intimate conversation with Sewell Satterfield.

"My office, tomorrow night at eight."

"Yeah. Sure. Whatever you say."

Later, on my way back to my room, I think about Caitlin Saunders wanting me to admit my anger with Mama, making me talk to a chair, making me beat a pillow around. Making me yell. And now I'm supposed to be *concerned* about Mama? Just when my anger is white-hot, I'm supposed to make this turnaround? And she's dragging Uncle Sewell into my therapy! It's embarrassing. Why not just pull a few people off the sidewalk? She pisses me off.

The door to my room is almost shut, and I kick it open with my foot. Someone on the other side lets out a surprised bleat. There's a new girl huddled on Rosmarin's bed, grasping a one-eyed teddy bear for protection. Besides the bear, her most identifiable feature is her short-cropped hair, which looks as if it's been cut with a Weedwacker.

"Oh," I say. "I didn't know anyone was here. I didn't mean to scare you." I try to smile. "I'm Hannah. Hannah Ziebarth."

She nods. She can only look at me in quick, terrified glances. She looks too young to be in here.

"What's your name?" I ask, sitting down on the desk chair nearer her bed.

"Tressa," she says.

Nurse Nancy appears at the door. "Oh, you're back," she says to me. "This is Tressa Braithwaite, your new roommate. Could you see that she gets in to dinner all right?"

"Sure," I say.

"You're in good hands," she says to Tressa, and leaves.

I do an emotional blink. I don't remember Nancy complimenting me before. I thought she didn't like me.

"We have a half an hour before dinner," I say to Tressa. I open the desk drawer and pull out Rosmarin's black nail polish. "Would you like me to paint your nails?"

"Okay," she says. Probably too afraid to say no. She gets up and sits across the desk from me.

It is when she stretches her hand across the desk that I see the deep bruises and welts on her upper arm.

That night in my journal, I write, "Mama has never come close to hitting me." It's not exactly what Caitlin is hoping for, but it's on my mind. Then I write, "Mama has a kind heart." I cross that out. I'm supposed to write about memories of Mama before Daddy died, but too much has happened since then. I can't even remember who I was before that happened.

Uncle Sewell comes dressed in a crisply ironed cowboy shirt and a bolo tie. His hair is wet, like he just showered and neatly parted it on one side and then combed it across the top of his head to cover the baldness. You'd think Aunt May would tell him that no one is fooled by this styling. He smells to high heaven of Old Spice. I think he might be even more nervous than I am.

"Hiya, Hannah." He grips my hand. "How ya doin'?"

"I'm okay." I smile big to put him at ease.

Caitlin invites him to sit in one of the three chairs in her office. His body takes up more than its share of the room.

"Thanks for coming, Sewell," Caitlin says, smiling. "Like I said on the phone, I think you might be able to help Hannah."

"Will if I can," he says, nodding. "Hannah's a good girl. A good worker." It sounds like a job reference.

I smile big again. This is so awkward. At least I'm medicated, I think. I'll bet Uncle Sewell would like something about now. It strikes me as a joke, and I giggle.

Uncle Sewell wipes his temples with a handkerchief he takes from his back pocket.

I imagine Caitlin handing him a sign with black lettering on it that says "Sewell" and making him hold it during the therapy. I giggle some more.

"I think Hannah is a very responsible person." Caitlin emphasizes *responsible* and I press my lips together to stop the giggling. She turns to me. "Hannah, do you want to tell Sewell what you'd like to know from him?

Huh? I'm surprised to be asked this. I thought she and Sewell would do the talking and I'd just sit and listen.

"Yeah, sure." I swallow. "Well, I'd like to know about Grandma Satterfield." I look at Caitlin to see if I'm heading in the right direction. She nods encouragement, and I proceed: "Mama always says I'm like Grandma. I've never been sure what that means. I was eight when Grandma died."

Uncle Sewell fidgets with his bolo tie. "You look like her, you know that?" He nods his head at me. "Your grandma was raised in Monroe. Her father was a clerk at the bank, and her mother was a housewife. She met Dad at a church dance over in Elsinore. He was teaching at the high school. I guess it was love at first sight, to hear her tell it. Anyway, they got married and had me six months later!" He laughs. "And I wasn't any preemie either." He slaps his stomach. "I was always big!"

I lean forward in my chair. "You're kidding! Grandma got pregnant before she was married?"

"Well, we never talked about it directly—she was pretty proper, you know, but I weighed eight pounds, ten ounces, so go figure!" He laughs again, his face red.

"Maybe it's hereditary," I say to Caitlin. "Maybe it's a recessive gene passed down—"

"I don't think so," Caitlin says.

Uncle Sewell is grinning like he told a dirty joke. He wipes his forehead. "Of course, she was out of high school then." The handkerchief returns to his back pocket.

"Does Mama know that Grandma got pregnant before she was married?" I ask.

"Oh, sure. She and I talked about it a couple of times." He turns to Caitlin. "When you're young, that sort of thing is mighty interesting." He chuckles.

"What else?" I ask. "About Grandma, I mean."

"Well, she was an artistic kind of person."

"You mean she painted?"

"No. More general than that. She liked to make things pretty. She dried flowers so that we had bouquets in the house all winter long—that sort of thing."

"Roses? Did she dry roses?"

"I'm not sure. I remember hydrangeas most particular. She belonged to a garden club. She developed some new varieties of iris. She liked all that gardening stuff. Mostly flowers. She did plant a vegetable garden, but that wasn't her first interest. The flowers was what she loved."

I try to remember Grandma's backyard, but no clear image appears.

"You dry roses, don't you, Hannah?" Caitlin asks.

"It's my passion," I say.

"So maybe your mother meant you were like your grandmother in that way?"

"Maybe—"

"But?" Her eyebrows are raised.

"Mama said that madness runs in families and skips generations. She said I was like Grandma Satterfield." I turn to Uncle Sewell. "Was Grandma crazy?"

He looks surprised. "Nora shouldn't say that. She knows better." He turns to Caitlin. "Hannah's mother, my sister, is deathly afraid of madness. You can't blame her, of course. She was just a little tyke when Mother was sick."

"Sick how?" Caitlin asks.

"Well, sick in the head, but it wasn't any hereditary thing. It was the disappointment, and probably it was chemical too. Anyway, it was that fool doctor's fault. She should have gone up to Salt Lake to have the surgery."

"What surgery? Was it brain surgery?" What kind of surgery would make Grandma sick in the head?

"No, no." He shakes his head. "When your mama was about three, our mother got appendicitis, and old Doc Cornwall, who, now that I think of it, never did make a correct diagnosis on anybody, said she needed her appendix out. Anyway, Mother has her appendix out in Doc Cornwall's office—he had a little surgery room off to the side—and that old fool decides to take her ovaries out as well. No warning. No consultation whatsoever. Just snips those suckers out!"

Caitlin covers her mouth with her hand.

"And he didn't give her any of those hormones or anything. She was despairing. Heck, it took her seven years to get pregnant with Nora after she had me, and she wanted a lot more children. Old Doc Cornwall ended all that. I don't know if it was the disappointment or if it was the hormonal changes that brought on the depression, but it was severe—lasted five years until Father took her to the L.D.S. Hospital up in Salt Lake and a specialist figured out what had happened. She got well almost immediately with the medication. Said it was like having a boulder lifted from her shoulders." He leans back in his chair. "But for five years, she didn't do anything but pick dust balls out of the carpet. I'm not kidding."

Caitlin shakes her head sympathetically. "Who took care of Nora, then?"

"Well, Father did the best he could. I watched her too, but I was only ten. I did teach her how to make those hollyhock dolls with the bonnets. You know, with toothpicks and all. But a lot of the time, she was alone with Mother. Mother's sister, Ida, would come in and check on her too during the day—made sure she got her lunch. Of course, later she was in school." Uncle Sewell clasps his hands and watches his twiddling thumbs. "It was a hard time for all of us, but I don't think Nora ever quite got over it."

I say, "No wonder Mama's never smiling in those old snapshots."

"There wasn't much to smile about, but listen, kiddo . . ." He grasps my hand. "It ain't catching, you know."

I squeeze his hand. "Tell me more about Grandma," I say.

Uncle Sewell likes his task and starts most of his sentences with, "I guess you know about the time when . . ." But every one of his stories is new to me. Does Mama even know these stories? Does she know how Grandma kept the family afloat by making and selling ice cream the summer Grandpa had rheumatic fever? How when she was young, Grandma and her sister, Ida, used to levitate their friends out on the picnic table in the back under the willow tree? "They had this little chant they'd say," Uncle Sewell says. "They could lift even big guys several inches off the table with just two fingers—"

"Grandma *levitated* people?"

Uncle Sewell chuckles. "They didn't have TV then, Hannah. They had to find something fun to do."

"But *levitation*!"

"Wish I could remember the chant." He grins.

When time is almost up, Uncle Sewell says he's glad to see me looking so well. "Bliss is expecting you when you're ready to start work again," he says.

I already know this, but I say, "Soon." We shake hands. Then I change my mind and hug him. "Thank you," I say. "Really, thank you."

When he's gone, I say to Caitlin, "I guess Mama talks about Grandma Satterfield in her therapy. I mean, she'd have to."

"Why do you say that?" she asks. She's taking her handbag out of her desk and turning off the desk light. It's the end of her work day, I realize.

"Because she's been mad at her for years without"—I

search for the right word—"without *examining* the reasons why. That kind of stuff can drive you crazy."

"It can and it does." Caitlin smiles and turns off the overhead light.

I walk out into the hall with her.

"We all have to make our peace with the preceding generations," she says. "Speaking of which—don't forget to write in your journal."

We're standing in front of the exit through which no mentally deranged adolescent can go without good behavior points, a pass, or an automatic weapon. The nurse pushes the buzzer, and Caitlin opens the door.

I clutch her arm. "Caitlin," I say. "How *is* Mama doing?"

She smiles a weary smile and pats my arm: "Mother and daughter are doing fine," she says. "We'll talk tomorrow."

"I don't have therapy tomorrow."

"On Thursday then. Good night." She disappears behind the door to her own life.

In the night I dream that Milo and Mimi marry at the high school. They are in full bridal dress, standing to their waists in the swimming pool in front of Mr. Layton, the band teacher, who is marrying them. All the kids, dressed in the usual baseball caps and jeans, sit in the bleachers on the side of the pool, hooting and hollering and stomping their feet for the ceremony to begin. I ask a strange girl next to me why they are marrying in water like this, and she says it's because Mimi is nine months pregnant and doesn't want anyone to know. When I look at Mimi again, the big balloon of her stomach has forced her back into the water so that she is floating on her back, her wedding gown spread out around her like the petals of a water lily. Milo holds her hand to keep her from floating away. Mr. Layton speaks the marriage vows and taps each of them on the shoulder with his baton and pronounces them man and wife. Then the double doors to the gym open wide, and Mama, holding a large silver platter of cookies, marches around the edge of the pool, saying, "I've brought you cookies." The kids cheer and the whole gym fills with a cookie chant. When Mama sees me, she comes directly to me and, leaning over me, says, "Look, alphabet letters!" Her eyes shine. The cookies, shaped like letters, are frosted in pastels and sprinkled with shiny candies. "They're your favorites," she says.

I wake up. "Mama," I whisper between gasps. My heart knocks unsteadily inside my sweaty T-shirt. "Mama!" It comes out in a whimper and I remember I have a roommate again. I look across at Tressa to see if she's heard me, but she's rolled into a ball around her one-eyed bear. I sit in the corner of my bed, hugging my knees, and let this lost memory consume me: Mama was everyone's favorite room mother, and it was because of the alphabet letter cookies. She baked a letter for each child—the letter that began his or her name. Each cookie was eight inches high. It took her a full day to make them. When I knew a class party was approaching, I'd ask her, "Will you make the alphabet letters?" And she'd say, "Of course, darling."

—————

Even though I'm shivering, I pull my diary out of the drawer next to the bed and turn on the tiny bedside lamp. I write it all down.

One memory follows another: Before he moves to West Jordan, Parker Shields breaks his arm flying off his garage with a red towel pinned to his neck. His mother isn't home, and Mama binds his arm in a dish towel and runs him to the emergency room of the hospital.

I walk with Mama around the neighborhood when she collects contributions for the American Cancer Society. She lets me wear all the little pins and takes them off one at a time as people contribute. I look like a war hero.

Mama is one of the chaperones when our fifth-grade class goes to visit the Hansen Planetarium.

I write it fast. All of it. All the evidence that Mama was a real mother to me before Daddy died. Mama was a presence. She and I finger painted with chocolate pudding at the kitchen table. Mama. I want my mama back.

In school the next morning, Link Bailey is missing. Axel says he's gone home, but Stephen says he heard two nurses talking and that Link Bailey tested positive for drugs. "They said he had the whole drugstore in him," Stephen says.

"How could he get it?" Lisa asks. "They watch your every move."

"His mother brought it in."

"His mother gave him drugs?" I am incredulous.

"Why are you so surprised?" Denay leafs through her notebook, looking for today's assignment. "We're all loaded down with our parents' junk. His is just more noticeable."

Mr. Dilworth, the teacher, walks in then with a quiz and starts passing it out.

I think about Denay's remark all morning. It isn't just Mama's fault that I'm in here. I made some of my own bad choices.

After lunch, Nancy comes to get me out of class. "Caitlin just called and said she forgot to tell you that she's arranged for you to be in the Teen Pregnancy Seminar today. It's being held down on the third floor. Come on, I'll take you down."

I'm a few minutes late and the presenter, Carla, who wears a name tag and has a precision haircut, has already begun. She stands in front of a table around which sit a half dozen girls about my age, a couple of them looking really pregnant. The rest look like me, virginal. I sit at the end of the table in the direct path of Carla's eye, so it seems she is talking to me and only to me. She spouts off facts that she gleans from a looseleaf in front of her: "There are twelve million sexually active teenagers in America; five million are female."

The arithmetic doesn't sound right and while I try to figure it out, I miss other essential facts about adolescent sexual activity. Isn't she talking to the wrong group? I keep looking at her, though, as if I'm paying attention, because she only looks at me.

"Thirty-five percent of teen pregnancies end in abortion."

Still the wrong group.

She lists off other statistics, and I'm a little steamed with Caitlin for setting this up for me. Carla says that only two to three percent of teen pregnancies become live births that are adopted. She follows that with, "Fewer than ten percent of babies born to teens are placed in adoptive homes."

Again the math seems off. She's talking so rapidly, I can't concentrate. Why is she rattling off these statistics?

I learn soon enough what the real subject of the hour is. She leans forward with hands on the table: "There are one million couples in the United States waiting to adopt a baby." Her voice has slowed down for emphasis. She wants this to sink in. "For every infant available, there are forty couples waiting to adopt."

I look away from her and see the book next to her loose-leaf, *The Adoption Reader*. At first I feel trapped and angry, but then Carla says she is not there to persuade us but merely to lay out some options for us.

I can handle this hour, I think. I have made up my mind already, and nothing she says will change it. I can handle this. I breathe in deeply and let the air out of my nose.

Did we know that we could choose the adoptive parents?

She picks up another fat loose-leaf with files of some of those million couples who want to adopt. "The overheads I'm going to show you are some of the files in this book, only the couples' surnames have been blacked out to protect their privacy." She turns on the overhead projector and turns off the lights. She lays on the first plastic sheet. It's Al and Ginny, last name blacked out, but their photograph in the corner dominates the page. Some privacy protection. I share a smirk with the girl sitting next to me. Al is a pediatrician and Ginny is a kindergarten teacher. We see Bill and Christine. He's a lawyer and she's a computer programmer. We see Phil and Luanne, both professors.

"Aren't there any bus drivers that want to adopt?" the girl up in front asks, and we all giggle out of caged nervousness.

"Adoptive parents are from all walks of life," Carla says with no detectable sense of humor. She looks through the plastic sheets. "Here's Ken and Ann. He's in construction, and she's a secretary." She keeps flipping through the overhead sheets so we can see the couples. My irritation dissolves into sadness to see those eager, smiling, thirty-something faces, so able in every way, except conception, hoping to be chosen like orphans in a home; while we, burdened with easy conceptions, stare back. Their faces haunt me for the rest of the day.

The next morning at breakfast, one of the nurses comes in to tell me there's a phone call for me. I have only received a couple of outside calls, from Trilby and the bishop, and they're always in the evening, so I'm pretty surprised. Walking into the hall, I wonder if it's Rosa Benson to tell me something's happened to Mama. It could happen. Things happen. They already have.

I pick up the phone at the nurses' station. "Hello," I say.

"Hannah? Oh, Hannah, honey, it's so good to hear your voice." She's breathless, like she's come from a distance, or like it took every megabyte of willpower to make this phone call.

"Mama? My gosh, Mama!"

The nurse at the desk smiles without looking up.

"Are you all right, Hannah? I mean—"

"Mama, you *called* me!"

"I did. I did it!" She laughs in a way I haven't heard for a long time. "I had to. I need to know how you are."

"I'm doing fine. I really am. It's helped to be here," I say. "I needed to be here, Mama." My eyes well up and I turn from the nurses' station and hug the wall. "What about you?"

"I'm better too." She sucks in her breath. She is trying not to cry. "I'm cooking again. The sisters at church just shop for me, but they don't have to cook for me anymore."

"Oh, Mama." Mama is calling me and I am blubbering against a wall.

"Do you have morning sickness?"

I shake my head and wipe my face with the palm of my hand. "No." It comes out a constricted shudder. "Mama."

"I'm getting better, Hannah. I'm going to be here for you. We're going to be okay." Her voice gets stronger as she speaks.

I nod and bawl silently into the phone.

She seems to know. "I don't want to lose you. She said I'd lose you if I didn't change. I don't want that, Hannah. I want to be your mother." She pauses. "I haven't ruined it between us, have I? Is it too late?"

"No, no," I quaver. "I need you to be my mother. You're the only mother I've got."

"Oh, sweetie."

"I love you, Mama."

"I love you too. Now I'm going—I know you have school—but I'll call you tonight again. I'll call you right at seven o'clock. You can expect it. Okay?"

"I can call *you*," I offer.

"No!" It comes out loud and determined as if she's resisting temptation. "No—*I* will call you. I *need* to call you."

"Okay," I say. "I guess I really need for you to call me." I give a half sob, half laugh.

"Yes, I think you do."

"I love you."

"I love you too. Until tonight."

"Bye."

That afternoon in my therapy session, Caitlin nods as I repeat my conversation with Mama. As always, she has a question for me: "Why did you offer to call her back?"

"Well, because I know how hard it is for her—"

She shakes her head. "You're very quick to step in for her."

"Well—"

"Let her be your parent, Hannah. She needs to be, and you need her to be."

I get it. I know what I do. I know how I contribute to what has become a problem with Mama: I'm too willing to take over her job, and since Daddy died, she has been willing to let me. "Daddy did it too, didn't he?"

"Yes, he was a white knight. You've learned from a master. Only it makes you sick. You still need mothering." She raises those eyebrows.

I start to cry again. It's a record day for it. "She was afraid of losing me. You told her it was a possibility, didn't you?"

Caitlin smiles. "She needed a nudge."

"Both of us needed a nudge."

"You were in big trouble," she says. "When you go home on Monday, you're going to have to be careful about your need to take care of her."

The room spins. "Monday? But that's just a few days away."

"August eighth, your sixteenth birthday. You can be home to celebrate it."

I stand up. "I'm not ready yet. I'm just catching on here. I'm not ready." I pace around the room.

"You're ready," she says.

"But we haven't talked enough about Milo. I mean, I'm such a pleaser, I was willing to believe he didn't mean to hit me . . ."

She turns in her chair to watch me pace around her desk. "You're only leaving the hospital, Hannah. You're not quitting therapy. We'll still meet together once a week, and we'll talk more about Milo. And we'll meet with your mother too." She smiles. "No more therapy with empty chairs."

She makes it sound so simple. "The baby. We haven't talked about the baby. I need lots of support here. I don't know what to do. I'm not sure that I know what a good decision is anymore. I thought I knew everything, but I don't." I grab her arm. "I have to stay here."

"Sit down, Hannah." She actually points to the chair. She moves her chair closer to mine so our knees touch.

"The more I hear you speak, the more convinced I am that you are ready to go home. What's more, your mother is ready to have you home. You have friends. You have all you need."

I rest my forehead on her knees. "I need you close by," I say. "I'm so afraid."

She strokes my hair. "I'll be here. What's more, I'll give you my home phone in case you have a crisis. I'm not going anywhere, Hannah. I'm not cutting you loose, but you don't need to be in a hospital anymore. It's okay to be afraid." She lets me cry for a long time.

At dinner I learn that Axel is also going home on Monday. "For good?" I ask.

"I'm staying on the medication this time," he says. "Maybe they'll let me drive a car. Then I could come and see you."

"You can see me before that. I already drive. I just have to get my license."

He laughs, a rare thing for Axel.

"Where do you live?"

"Up by the capitol."

"I'll come and get you."

"Come and get us too," Lisa says. "We can all run away from home."

I look at my plate. I have eaten one hundred percent of my dinner. "I don't want to run away from home," I say.

Mama calls me right at seven. I tell her I remember the eight-inch letter cookies. She says she will make some.

Sunday we party a good part of the day with a picnic in Millcreek Canyon. The mountains make us feel alive and whole. We exchange little presents, all of them nonglass, nonsteel, noncombustible. Stephen shows us how we can commit suicide and have a high at the same time by trying to snort a Beanie Baby up his nose. It's the first time I've ever seen him make a joke.

Mama calls me on Sunday night. She says she has called Rosa Benson and asked her to pick me up in the morning.

"You really can call out!" I exclaim.

"Yes," she says. "I can call out."

It is a dazzling, bright day when Rosa Benson drives me home in her Blazer. I hold the lavender and perfect Intermezzo that she has brought for me. "This is my favorite of all your roses."

She smirks as she turns the corner onto E Street.

"Don't I know it," she says. "Are you continuing your life of crime?"

"Not if you're going to be a good sport about it."

We ride in a comfortable silence for several minutes, but when we turn onto 9th South, she says, "Hannah, before we get home, I want you to know that I would be happy to help you with anything."

"Thank you," I say automatically.

"I mean"—she swallows—"even with the baby. If you need help with the care of the baby, I would be happy to help."

I turn to look at her then. "You would do that?"

"Yes. You just ask. Okay?"

I nod. She continues to surprise me. I thought she was such a crotchety old biddy. I have to rethink everyone. That is Milo's gift to me.

McClelland Street is green with overgrown trees whose roots have buckled the sidewalks. The sloping lawns on the east side all seem newly cut for my arrival home. It is still a beautiful street, despite Mr. Knight's backhoe. The car stops directly in front of my house and there, across the white stucco porch, is strung a ribbon of very large cookie letters that read, "Happy Birthday, Hannah."

Even before Rosa beeps the horn, Mama, grinning nervously, opens the door and steps out on the porch. I can't keep my chin from quivering as she moves quickly down the stairs. I open the door and run to meet her at the top of the slope. "Mama," I cry.

"Happy birthday!" she whispers into my neck.

We laugh and bawl at once, and Rosa Benson, who is pulling my suitcase out of the back of the Blazer, gives Mama a thumbs-up sign with one hand. Mama pulls me down the second set of stairs to the sidewalk and grabs Rosa's hand. "I did it. I did it."

The three of us are connected at the hands in a circle, and Rosa lifts our arms to the sky and lets out a celebratory howl. If we are not trembling with anxiety, then we must be dancing. It *feels* like dancing, although to anyone else our yowling and stomping may look just plain crazy.

❀

❀

❀

PART IV

Roman Speaks

I'm the next Tiger Woods. That's what my father says as my brother Milo and I wait to watch the play-off between Tom Lehman and Tiger Woods in the Mercedes-Benz Golf Classic, the new year's first pro golf tournament. It's the last round of the week, and it's raining in Carlsbad, California, where the game is supposed to be played, and doesn't look like it will stop for forty days and forty nights. Some of the greens are flooded over. The sportscasters have a couple of hours to fill, and nothing's happening. They talk about the weather and show tapes from the day before.

"He reminds me of you," my father says when Woods makes an eagle to tie Lehman. "That's the way you pulled it out last year at that meet in St. George." His fingers play nervously with the sleeve on the sofa arm.

"I wasn't playing fourteen below par," I say. My father misses essential information when it comes to his sons. Like he doesn't notice that Milo is barely watching TV. I mean, his eyes are on the screen, but that glazed look tells me he's got other things on his mind.

"But you hang in there," my father continues, "and you stay calm when you're behind. You don't give up. That's what it takes—that kind of tenacity." He hits the sofa arm with a balled fist. "In a couple of years they'll be comparing you to Tiger Woods."

In your dreams.

Milo's jaw muscle flexes. It's the only clue to how tense he is. He lies back on the sofa, his feet spread across the new coffee table. My mother would freak if she saw those soccer cleats on that table, even if she did pay a bundle for that "distressed" look. But my mother has taken Tony and the girls off for a few days of skiing in Park City, so they won't know that our family has any difficulties. If we look good, we are good. That's my mother's philosophy. Hannah's lawyer friend called yesterday, and she knew he would call again, and that could only mean trouble.

On the television, Woods comes out under a Titleist umbrella, hands it to someone, and begins warming up. Lehman wins the toss, so he will go first. The announcers reflect with each other over the advantages of being first.

My father says, "You never have to worry about money again when you're that good." *He* worries about money a lot.

"Guess not," I say.

"If Tiger Woods wins this, he'll have made over a million in winnings in his rookie year."

I nod. I already know this. Everyone in the world knows it. Shut up, I want to say. Shut up about Tiger Woods and money. Why don't we talk about the really big news of the day, which doesn't happen to be Tiger Woods's performance at the Mercedes-Benz Golf Classic. Let's talk about how we're all nervous about this call for Milo to go to the hospital and give a blood sample for DNA testing to prove he's not the father, and you're not the grandfather, and I'm not the uncle of that baby that's being born today, maybe this very minute. Let's talk about how you're afraid Milo may have been lying all this time. How about that for a lively conversation?

Lehman is at the seventh hole, ready to start. The camera pans across a small lake, and the announcers declare that his job is to get the ball across the lake into good position. To put pressure on Tiger Woods.

I wonder if sportscasters struggle with suicide daily, having to say the obvious like that. Must feel like having a chicken carcass stuck in your throat.

Lehman swings and we watch the ball rise and arc wide, but not wide enough. It plunges into the water. "Ohhhh," my father and I moan. He curses.

"What happened?" Milo asks, his eyes focused on the TV for the first time.

"Lehman hit it in the lake!" I say. Lehman's face is so miserable, I want to cry. He boofs it in the playoff round! I yank my hair up from my scalp in frustration for him.

"Geez, I can play better than that," Milo says.

Dork. "So can he," I say.

"That's the game, right there." My father scoops up some chips and guacamole dip my mother made and crams them into his mouth.

Tiger Woods is tall, elegant, and handsome in black. He's everything I'm not. He's cool to the tip of his Nike cap. He scans the fairway looking for mythic lakes and bunkers. He clasps the seven iron, but still takes his time, looking, imagining the perfect drive. He swings. The camera follows the ball into the air. My father and I react with the television crowd as the ball drops onto the green and rolls within seven inches of the hole. We let out a whoop.

"Shhh," Milo says.

"Just when you think this young man has done it all . . . ," the announcer starts up.

"Turn it down," Milo says.

When I do, we can all hear it: the phone is ringing.

"I'm not answering," Milo says.

"Get it," my father says to him. It's not a tone he usually takes with Milo, his favorite son.

Milo doesn't hurry.

My father and I turn back to the TV. Tiger Woods almost grimaces, walking in the rain to the putting green. Maybe it's his way of being modest, but he doesn't smile until he makes the putt and the crowd goes crazy.

I can hear Milo's voice say a series of "yeahs." And then, "What floor did you say?" Pause. "I don't have to see Hannah, do I? Because after the things she said about me, I don't want to—"

"You're as good as Tiger Woods, and you only have one eye!" My father actually says this. "First thing is to get you into Stanford. They've got the best golf program in the country."

I nod. Maybe I could fall off another cliff and lose an arm, then I could be a one-armed, one-eyed Tiger Woods.

I hear Milo hanging up. Tiger Woods is hugging his parents.

"They want me now," Milo growls from the kitchen.

My father jumps up, turns off the TV, and motions for me to get up too. "Come on," he says, "he needs our support."

He doesn't bother asking the sex of the baby, but I want to know. "What is it?"

"A boy," Milo says, opening the front door. "Not that it matters, because it isn't mine." He's been saying this since last August when Hannah filed a paternity suit against him, but I'm the only one in the family who doesn't believe him. Even that night when I saw Hannah, her face all swollen, lying in the back of the 4Runner—I suspected. When I heard she really was pregnant, I knew for sure he had done that to her. No girl is going to stop Milo's brilliant career. Milo will see to it and so will my parents. We Fabianos will stand together through Hannah's paternity suit. All she wants is for Milo to admit that he is the father and to sign off his rights to the child so that she can put it up for adoption. My father is sure she wants money. He and Milo tell everyone they know that Hannah was sleeping with at least five other guys at the time. They even name names: Fishbeck and Neal Garrett both say they've slept with her.

What time was he born, this baby who is flesh of our flesh? How many hours old is he? These are not questions I'm allowed to ask.

We take Milo's 4Runner, because it has the TV set on a screwed-in panel on the dashboard so we can watch the closing moments of the tournament. Tiger Woods is handing the keys of a new Mercedes to his mother. "In a couple of years," my father's saying, "they'll be following Roman Fabiano around like that, and you'll be handing the keys of that Mercedes over to *your* mother." He is driving; I'm in the passenger seat, and Milo sits behind in the middle.

"Cool," I say. I've decided not to create waves with the parents. They get all hysterical if you deviate from their plans for you, but when I'm eighteen, I get some money put in trust for me by my grandfather, and then I'm heading for Arizona, where I'm going to school to major in sports psychology and to play golf. I'm not going to be a professional golfer, and I'm not going to Stanford. I'm going to train golfers to get their heads straight for winning, and in my spare time I'll play golf for the sheer joy of playing. My father will freak. It doesn't make enough money. It isn't glamorous enough, but I don't want to be my parents' pet monkey, performing my little tricks so they can brag to their friends.

"You just need to take the initiative, son," my father is saying.

"I know." I lift my eyebrows, hoping to look enthusiastic, because if I don't, he'll yell about what a sloth I am, how I won't take responsibility for my life. It's the kind of speech he gives in capital letters with enough exclamation marks to choke a word processor.

He reaches over and pats my knee. "You could learn a thing or two from Milo—he goes after what he wants."

I should yell now or hit him, but I'm afraid I'd kill him with one blow. He's always setting up Milo as the perfect example of what I should be. Milo is outgoing. Milo participates in school sports. Milo runs for office and wins. Milo dates real lookers. Milo. Milo. Milo.

Milo gets Hannah pregnant. Why don't I get some nice girl pregnant and then beat her up when she tells me? I can still see Hannah's face trying to hide under that blanket in the 4Runner. I said her name, "Hannah," just under my breath. A hot shame radiates out from my belly when I remember Hannah. Shame that I'm too weak to defend her. Shame for my family, who thinks dollars can buy anything and anybody.

I'm always losing my sunglasses and now, sitting in the front seat without them, with the sun glaring off the hood into my eyes, I'm getting a headache. I cup one hand over my forehead and look out the side window as we pass the Smith's Food King on E Street. They sell flowers there. I think of taking Hannah flowers. What would I say to her? Take my flowers? Forgive me for being a Fabiano? Thank you for making me an uncle? Will you marry me?

My ears heat up from daring even to think that last

question. As if she'd want a golf dweeb on Accutane to clear up his zits. As if she'd want any Fabiano now.

I'd change my name for you, Hannah Ziebarth. Marry me.

I shake my head. *Stop thinking. Stop.*

Outside, the leftover snow from Christmas is dirty, so that even though the sun is shining, the winter landscape is depressing.

"Okay, this is it," my father says as he pulls into the parking garage.

"I'm not seeing her," Milo says.

"You won't have to," my father says.

But at the reception desk of the hospital, they direct him to the maternity ward on the third floor.

"No way." Milo throws up his hands. "I'm outta here." He turns to leave, but my father clutches his arm.

"Just hold up while we get this straightened out," he says.

I'm standing behind the two of them, but I can see the receptionist, a grandmother type, watching our little family drama over the top of her reading glasses.

My father turns to her, still grasping Milo. "Look, it's just a blood test he needs to take—it's a delicate matter. Couldn't they take a blood test on some other floor in the hospital?"

Grandmother type—her name tag says *Ethella*—picks up the phone and asks somebody the same question. She's put on hold.

Milo complains, "Geez, why don't I just cut open a vein right here and be done with it?" He blows air through his lips.

"Yes?" says Grandma Ethella into the phone. "Good, I'll tell him." She smiles, happy to be the bearer of good news. "You can go to the fourth floor nursing station in the west wing." She points to the elevators.

My father moves out with Milo at his side. I stay back. "I think I'll wait here for you," I say. I point to the magazines on the table. "They've got a *Golf Digest* I haven't seen yet."

"We won't be long," my father calls, already halfway to the elevators. Even from where I'm standing I can see that muscle in Milo's cheek flexing like he's biting a bullet.

When they're safely on the elevator, I head down the main hall past the gift shop and the pharmacy and look for the stairs. They're not hard to find, and I take them two at a time to the third floor. The door from the stairwell leads into a well-lighted hallway across from a nurses' station. I don't know where I'm going exactly—that is I, *do* know where I'm going, I just don't know how to get there—so I turn right only because I don't have to cross directly in front of the two nurses sitting at the desk. I walk like Tiger Woods, like I know where I'm going. Then I see the sign: Nursery, with an arrow pointing left. There it is, a whole wall of windows filled with clear plastic bassinets. I stand at the intersection of two hallways. From here I can see that only some of the bassinets have babies in them. They're wrapped in either pink or blue blankets. A man and a woman stand at the corner farthest away from me, smiling down at a pink shape. Besides them, there is one nurse in the nursery, but I can't see anyone else. Figuring it's safe, I move to the windows and look inside. The last names of the babies are printed with a black marker on a card and attached to the top of each bassinet. Baby Crenshaw. Baby Nagel. Baby Lancaster. Baby Wong. Four boy babies. No Ziebarth baby.

"Have you got a relative in here?" the man at the window asks.

My voice cracks when I blurt out, "No!" It's too loud. I soften my voice: "I mean yes."

He chuckles. "Which is it?"

"I'm a first-time uncle." I try to regain that Tiger Woods composure, but I can tell by his amused look that I'm coming off more like Fozzie Bear.

"We just had our first grandchild—Tiffany." The woman says. "She's such a sweetie."

I look where she's looking. Sweetie has inherited somebody's awful nose. She's looks like an old man. "Yeah," is all I can say.

"Where's your—"

"He's not here," I say, looking again.

"A nephew!" the man exclaims. "Well, that's terrific."

"He's probably with his mother," the woman says.

"Oh, yeah, sure . . ." I head off down a hallway. "I'll go see her, ah, my sister, that is." Any minute I'll start drooling. I sound so stupid. I need rehearsals for this kind of thing.

I'm heading the opposite way from where I came in, but at the far end of the hall I see an exit sign. How lost can I be? Some of the doors are partly open, and I see mothers and fathers and babies or women just napping. I don't belong here.

"How long will he be?" I hear a tearful voice ahead of me. "I really want to be with him while I can." If I'd been walking any faster I would have collided with a bassinet on wheels coming out of room eighteen. It is pushed by a nurse, with Hannah in a robe, her face blotchy, behind her. It takes only a millionth of a second for me to realize this and I turn around immediately and walk back in the direction of the nursery.

"I only need to draw a little blood, and then I'll bring him right back," the nurse says. "Go lie down for a few minutes. You haven't slept since you had this baby!" Her voice is friendly. "Go on," she chides.

I didn't expect Hannah would be up. Can women just walk around after they've had a baby? Don't they have to stay in bed or something?

To my relief, the couple that was standing at the nursery window is now gone. I turn the corner and stand against the wall. The back of my T-shirt is wet with nervous sweat. I bend over and rub my face with both hands, listening to the wheels of the bassinet approaching and the nursery door opening. When I peek around the corner, Hannah is not in sight. The nurse leaves "Baby Ziebarth" right in front of the window and goes looking for something. The other nurse is feeding one of the babies in an incubator. It's only a few steps to the window and I'm looking down at Hannah's baby, who is actually awake. His eyes, dark and wide-set like Milo's, look up at the lights while his tiny body writhes like a kitten's. His hands are covered with the sleeves of his undershirt, so I can't see his fingers. I remember that Rose and Gina had long, wrinkled little fingers that would wrap around my pinky when they were brand new. I lean my head against the window and he yawns and blinks his eyes. The inside of his mouth is the cleanest pink; his tongue curls under. He has a perfectly round head and better color than any of the other babies. I mean, people say all babies look alike, but they don't. This baby doesn't have a nose that looks like the end of a watering can, for one thing. And he doesn't have one of those coneheads. He has soft, dark hair.

He smiles! He smiles at me with Fabiano dimples. It's more than gas, I'm sure of it.

I smile back and give him a little wave. There's nobody watching, and who cares even if there is. *Hi, baby. Hi, you sweet baby.* I'm pressed against the glass, not wanting to leave and knowing I have to soon. A strong emotion catches me in the back of the throat and I have to work hard to keep from sobbing. *You are one sweet baby.*

The nurse comes back. I back away from the window. "It's okay," she says. "I just need to draw some blood." She holds up a needle. "He won't like it, though." Her voice is muffled through the glass. She unwraps the blue blanket and jabs one scrawny foot.

The baby yowls his outrage. His head turns red, and his free leg flails while the nurse pinches the blood from his foot into a rubber tube. When he turns his head, I see a tiny muscle flex with tension on the side of his jaw.

I've been away too long and turn to find the exit leading to the stairwell. His wailing fills the hallway. Only when I close the door behind me and I'm on the stairs does it stop.

You're a part of our family, I think. I don't need a DNA test to know that. *You're family.* At the first-floor landing, I sit on the bottom stair and press the palms of my hands against my eyes. I guess I cry for the baby that I'll never know, but I'm crying for myself too, because lately I haven't felt like I have anything in common with anyone else in my family. My mother can hardly look at me. My face bothers her: "Try to look straight at people, or they won't know which eye to look at," she says. "Have you taken your Accutane? You seem to be breaking out again," or "Honey, stand up straight, so those bony wings don't poke out so much." Both my parents are good looking and so are their children, except me. Both parents are accomplished and smooth and so are their children, except me. The whole family is totally upscale. Except me. I don't really care about upscale.

But the thing is—and this is so funny—that Milo's baby is everything they'd want—he's beautiful. He'd fit in better than I do, and I'm the only one who knows it. Both the baby and I are on the outside. It makes me want to laugh. It makes me want to cry, which is what I'm doing.

When I can stop sobbing, I wipe my face with the

bottom of my T-shirt and run my fingers through my hair a couple of times. Taking a deep breath, I step into the corridor. On the wall are framed photographs of men who have donated money to the hospital. I head back to the reception area, where my father sits with a glowering Milo.

"Sorry," I say. "I had to go to the bathroom."

My father stands. "We just barely got back," He scrutinizes my face. "You okay? Your face is red."

"Accutane face." Milo snorts.

"Better than pizza head, though," I say.

His lips curve up slightly. "For sure," he says. It's the first sign of any humor he's shown all day. I guess having the blood test over with is a relief. He's wearing a Band-Aid on the inside of his elbow.

"When will they know?" I ask. We're heading out the front door of the hospital. The air is cold, the sky clear.

"Three or four days," my father says. "It'll come out negative, and then I guess she'll have to start pulling in all those other guys she's been diddling. Her lawyer will be rich."

I wince. "Hannah's not like that," I can't help saying.

Milo and I share a look; he turns away first.

"Well, she's certainly taken your brother for a ride, that's all I can say. But there's no arguing against DNA testing." My father unlocks the car door.

I get in the front seat and wonder if he'll hold to that opinion when the results come in.

On the day before we go back to school from the Christmas vacation, our family always goes to the

Game Street Galleria to "play." This got started when Milo and I were in grade school and we got to pick what we wanted to do. We picked the Game Street Galleria, and it's stuck ever since, much to my mother's annoyance, since she hates the place, with its gigantic bowling alley, batting cages, video games, miniature golf, and every other distraction for young minds. "It smells like cheap pizza," she always says. She tries to divert us with new ideas: how about a day and a night at the Homestead? They have a swimming pool. So do we, we say. How about a cultural day? We can visit a museum, go to the ballet or the symphony. Bronx cheers from everybody. The only year her diversion worked was when she got Jazz tickets for everyone, but today the Jazz don't play, and besides, Gina and Rose decided that being at a basketball game wasn't all that interesting after the first five minutes. The one rule for this day is that the whole family is required to go. No excuses.

"Let's bowl first this time," Rose says as we all climb into the Suburban. She's clutching her Jo doll from *Little Women.*

"Bowling is last," my father says. "After dinner."

My mother adjusts the heater and says, "I read somewhere that the worst place for picking up every bacteria known to man is in the holes of a bowling ball." She holds out her manicured fingers and shudders. "Ooh."

Milo and I imitate the skittish movement of her hands and in falsetto voices cry, "Ooooh."

She turns in her seat and smacks both of our legs playfully. "You guys! You know it's true." She looks at me and smiles. "Your face is all cleared up. It looks really good." My mother is beautiful when she smiles. She digs around in her purse and hands back some lip balm. "Put this on your lips. They're dried and cracking."

Clear face, cracking lips. It's never quite right. "It's the Accutane," I say, but I smear some on to please her. Everyone is in a good mood, and I want to have it last a little while. The mailman came at lunch, and Milo and I got notices that we both made honor roll last semester. That kind of news acts as amphetamines for my parents. Zing. Their offspring are climbing the ladder of success. We are a united Fabiano front. Watch our dust.

I make a decision that today, at least, I'll try to forget it's all going to blow up in their faces.

Tony plays minesweeper on his Game Boy. Static, tinny explosions rise from his hands when he hits a mine, followed by "Gosh, darn it." Rose and Gina sing "Ninety-nine Bottles of Beer on the Wall," and judging from the roadblocks along I-15, they may make it to zero. Even Milo, who must know what's coming, seems relaxed. He sings with the girls but stammers all the *b* words, so that they break into giggles and can't decide whether it should be ninety-six or ninety-five bottles now.

My mother and father murmur about traffic to each other, and frequently my mother reaches over and massages the back of my father's neck. For a few minutes, anyway, we're a happy family.

Past 21st South we finally get some speed. I look out

the window, westward, trying not to think of Hannah and Milo's baby but not being very successful. The Oquirrh Mountains in the distance are a blurred purple with snowy tops, the sky a polluted blue gray. My warm breath condenses on the frosted window, and I start wiping at it when I'm jolted out of my little reverie by a billboard. I have to turn my head to read it all. It's a young woman holding a baby under her chin, her lips touching the top of its head, and it reads, "I love my baby enough to give him the life he deserves."

My head whirls with questions: Who is the ad for? A billboard on the interstate. I wish I could have read the rest of it.

"Don't bite your lips, Roman. It will make them bleed," my mother says over her shoulder. "Put on more lip balm if they bother you."

I nod and pull the tube out of my pocket. She'll have me applying it every five minutes.

For the rest of the day, I can't shake off that billboard. Skee-Ball, pool, miniature golf don't erase its ambiguous message. Even when I'm bowling the best game I've ever played, that line, "I love my baby enough . . ." flits in and out of my head like unwanted images in a dream.

It's after eight before we go home. On the way out to the parking lot, I decide to see if the same sign is posted on the opposite side of the highway. Snow is falling when I carry Gina piggyback to the Suburban. Rose is asleep on my father's shoulder. Tony is counting up tickets he won in Skee-Ball. "I'm saving them up for a year so I can get a really good prize," he says. Never mind that he's only out there once a year. I make sure I get a window seat on the right side so I can look for the billboard. The ride home is quiet, except for a low, humming beat from the music Milo's listening to on his headphones. My father drives cautiously through the increasing snowfall. I peer through the glass, surveying each lighted billboard as it whisks by, trying to look ahead slightly so I'll have time to read all the print when the one I want shows up again.

And then I see it: "I love my baby enough to give him the life he deserves." Even when I'm concentrating as hard as I can, it's impossible to read the smaller print, but I do get the words *Adoption Agency*. Some adoption agency is advertising for babies? They can do that? I substitute *mother* for *baby* to see how that works: "I love my mother enough to give her the care she deserves," maybe advertised by an elderly care center. How about "I love my kidney enough to give it the life it deserves," advertised by Sell Your Body Parts Clinic?

The billboard makes me mad. Oh, yeah, I understand that an older, more mature couple with money can give Hannah and Milo's baby a good home, can love it as much as Hannah must love it, judging from the teary voice I heard in the hospital wanting that baby back as soon as possible, holding him until she can't anymore.

I know why I'm mad. I want to hold the baby too. I want to be his uncle. I seem to be the only one in the family who even wants to consider that he is our relation. If only Hannah had fallen for me. If only, if only. Fat chance, next to Milo.

My mother strokes the sleeping Gina's head, which is pressed against her shoulder. Won't she want to know her grandson?

When we arrive home, the twins wake up while their parkas are being removed. "Now are we going to have the root beer floats?" Rose asks, taking my father's hand.

"Yes, now it's root beer float time!" Gina makes a leap across the kitchen floor.

My mother, her face strained from the long day of "fun," says, "Oh, I forgot to buy root beer." She opens the refrigerator door and then the pantry. "Only ginger ale." She glances at her watch. "It's so late. Why don't we have floats tomorrow night? You have school in the morning."

Rose and Gina line up together as only twins can do, both their faces held on "plea." Rose says, "But we always have the root beer floats after—"

"It's a transition!" Gina says.

"Tradition," my father corrects her.

"I'll go get root beer," Milo says, pulling car keys out of his pocket. "You guys get the ice cream in the glasses," he says to the girls, "and give me the most."

"Yeah!" The girls giggle.

"I'll go with you," Tony says. He shoves the Game Boy in his pocket. They leave, and I get the glasses down.

The girls sit on the bar stools, twirling around, laughing when their knees touch. My mother opens the ice cream. "It's frozen hard," she says to my father. "Do you mind scooping?"

He sticks the half gallon into the microwave and turns it on.

"Coward," my mother says.

The phone rings and I pick it up. "Fabiano's Ice Cream Parlor," I say. "May I take your order?"

The twins squeal and cup their hands over their mouths. My father rolls his eyes.

"This is Bill Kelsey," the voice at the other end says. "I'll take anything chocolate."

"Oh, sorry, Mr. Kelsey. We're just making root beer floats here—"

"Sounds great. Is this Milo?"

"No, it's Roman. Milo's out right now."

"Is your dad home?"

"Yeah, sure." I cover the mouthpiece. "He wants to talk to you." I hold the phone out to my father.

"He must have gotten the DNA report," my father says, crossing the room.

My mother gathers the twins nervously. "Come on," she says. "Let's put on your pajamas and then Milo will be back with the root beer."

The girls squiggle out of the room, poking one another, my mother behind them, directing them to the stairs.

My father waits until they are out of hearing. "This is Frank Fabiano," he says.

I take the ice cream out of the microwave. It is still hard, but I begin spooning some into a glass.

"Yes, we were gone all day," my father says, and then, "Oh? How did it come out?" His voice is controlled. There is no sign of the irritation I know he feels toward Mr. Kelsey and the whole DNA test.

"What?" his head jerks up, more attentive. "That's not possible." Pause. "Well, the lab obviously made a mistake!"

I stop scooping.

My father paces the length of the telephone cord. "I see," he says. "I suppose the girl wants money . . ."

Her name is Hannah. Call her Hannah.

"What do you mean?" He runs his fingers through his hair nervously. "That's it?" He seems stunned. "When?" And finally, "Yeah. That's it, then? She can't bring another suit against him later for emotional damage or some damn thing? Yeah. Okay. Yes. Yes. He'll be there." He doesn't say good-bye, just hangs up the phone and curses.

"I guess the test came out positive," I say quietly.

He nods.

We hear Milo and Tony laughing even before the back door opens. "Yo ho, everybody. We've got root beer. We went to Hires and got the good stuff, instead of—"

My father's grim face stops him midsentence. "What?" he says.

"Geez, did somebody die?" Tony asks.

"Tony, will you take this out to the trash?" My father hands him a small bag from under the sink.

"You're trying to get rid of me, aren't you?" Tony says.

"Just take it," my father says.

207

"I'm almost as old as Roman. I know stuff." But he can see from my father's face that he's not giving in. "Geez," he says under his breath.

When Tony's out the door, my father says, "The DNA test came out positive."

"That's not possible!" Milo steps forward. "Dad, I never slept with her. She's trying to ruin me just because I broke up with her. She's crazy, Dad. Really crazy."

We hear the twins babbling on the stairs. My father holds up his hand. "Later," he says to Milo.

The girls run in, their identical flowered nightgowns fluttering around their bare feet. Tony returns. Sullen at being forced out, he plops down in the family room and turns on the TV.

My father and mother share one of those knowing looks. So now we have to act the happy family for the girls' sake, and we do this depressingly well. My father makes the floats fizzy at their request, and Milo twirls the girls on the bar stools while they wait. I sit next to my mother, who looks bemused. "Want me to twirl you?" I ask her.

"I'd throw up." She smiles. I have the feeling she wants to throw up anyway.

The girls request straws.

"No straws tonight," my father says. "We don't have time for a lot of foolery." He's referring to Rose and Gina blowing bubbles into the root beer floats and never getting around to actually eating any of them. He sounds curt, and Rose asks," Are you mad?"

His face relaxes. "No, Rose, I'm just tired." He rubs

his forehead with his fingers. "Just tired." We all look into our floats. Mine is half gone and I don't remember tasting any of it. Milo sits with his lips pursed in thought.

The girls chatter constantly. The rest of us only talk in response to them. What we really want to discuss has to wait until they're gone.

Finally my mother says, "Okay, young ladies, time for bed. Put the glasses by the sink and hurry upstairs."

"Can't we stay up a little longer?" Rose begs.

"No, not tonight. You have school tomorrow, and it's already past your bedtime. Besides, you've had a fun day, haven't you?"

"I liked the Skee-Ball," Gina says.

"Me too!"

"Go on up," my mother says. "I'll come tuck you in a minute." She remembers Tony. "You too, Tony."

"I'm not finished with my float yet." He's slouched low in the armchair.

"Tony!" My father's voice is stern.

Still Tony doesn't hurry. He stands, still slouching, his lips contorted in rebellion. "Geez, can't I even finish my float?" He puts the glass down on the new coffee table, but my parents are so eager to be rid of him, neither one of them comments.

My mother follows him to the stairs and watches him go up. "Don't forget to brush your teeth," she calls. Then she's back in the kitchen. "The test was *positive?*" Her voice is high, incredulous. She looks at Milo. "How could that be? The two of you were only together in groups!" She had seen to that.

"That's just it," Milo says. "It's *not* possible. She's just a psycho."

"Can't we have our own test run at another lab? There could be a mistake. It happens," my mother says.

"They've already run the tests at two different labs," my father says. "Kelsey anticipated us there. As far as any court is concerned, Milo is the father of that girl's baby."

"What does she want?"

"She's not getting anything—" Milo's practically spitting.

"Apparently she doesn't want money," my father says. "She wants Milo to sign a waiver giving up any rights to the child. He can do that tomorrow in Kelsey's office."

"She doesn't want money?" My mother is baffled. "But why?"

Milo's face is tight, a tiny vein throbs in his forehead. "That's like saying I'm guilty!" His voice is sharp. "Everyone at school will know. The teachers—the students—everyone will know!"

Exactly, I think. Hannah is brilliant. She brought the paternity suit against Milo so people would know the truth.

Cursing, he throws the root beer glass into the sink, where it shatters.

"Milo!" My mother jumps.

"Well?" Milo shouts. "She's ruining my whole senior year! What are my teachers going to think? Maybe they'll retract their letters of recommendation."

They'll also know he beat her up.

I wait for my parents to confront Milo with the incongruities between his claims and the facts of two positive DNA tests and Hannah's only demand: his signature.

No one speaks. The ice maker in the refrigerator turns on, humming steadily. My father plays with his left ear, thinking. My mother's head is bowed, and she has both arms pulled tight into her body, clenched fists under her chin. For the first time, there are strain lines between her eyes.

"This doesn't have to ruin everything," my father says to Milo, grasping his shoulder.

"You don't think?" my mother asks.

"No, he can go away until it's time for college—I have a friend who's a headmaster at a prep school in California, where Milo can—"

I can't believe my ears. "What?" It comes out as a shout. "You're kidding, aren't you?"

"Why would I be kidding?" my father says. "I'm not going to have some low-life girl destroy my son's life."

"What about Hannah's life? Have you given a second's thought to that? What about what Milo has done? Doesn't it bother you that he's—that, that . . ." My face burns and I'm afraid I'm going to cry, but it doesn't matter anymore. "Doesn't it bother you that he's brought a life into the world and that he's acting so—so irresponsibly?"

"You shut up!" Milo's fist is clenched.

"You know you did," I shout at Milo. "And what's more, you beat her up when she told you!"

"Don't, don't!" My mother covers her ears and turns away.

Milo lunges for me, knocking me against the pantry door. "Shut up. Shut up!"

"I saw her that night." I'm panting. Milo's ten times stronger than I am, and he has me pinned with his body, taking punches at me wherever he can get them in. "She was hiding in the back of the 4Runner when you took Mimi home."

He flinches. He's hearing this for the first time.

"Her eye was swollen shut and there was blood all around where you hit her."

He punches me hard in the gut, and I fall to the floor, the wind knocked out of me. "I said shut up, you liar!" He kicks me in the leg.

"Boys!" my father shouts.

"Frank, do something," my mother says. "I can't have this!"

With my first return gasp of air, I hurl myself at Milo's legs as hard as I can. He falls sideways, his shoulder and head thudding against the refrigerator door. "Shut up yourself!" I gasp. I'm on top of him before he has time to know where he is. I swing at his face. "Is this how you smashed her? Did it feel good? It feels good to me." My fists rage at his face and don't stop even when the blood gushes from his nose. "How does it feel, Milo? How does it feel?" I will kill him and not be sorry.

"I'm not listening to this. I'm not!" My mother rushes for the stairs, hands still cupped over her ears.

My father's arm locks around my throat and drags me off, but Milo gets a few good kicks in with his boot.

"That's out of line, Roman. You're way out of line!" my father shouts at me.

I jerk free of his arm. "*I'm* out of line? What about your glory-boy here? Haven't you heard anything?"

My father turns away and looks through the window out to the backyard, where the patio light shows the snow falling thicker now. "We'll give Hannah all the money she needs," he says softly.

Something—a laugh, a sob, I'm not sure which—shudders out of me. "That's not the point. Hannah's never wanted your money."

"Well, then, what the hell is the point?" He's weary now of dealing with my questions.

"The point is that there is a baby—I saw him, a boy, your grandson. He looks just like our family. The point is, Milo beat up a nice girl!"

"You saw the baby?" This is my father.

"You had no right," Milo says.

"When did you—you didn't go see that girl?" My father can't believe it. He hands Milo wet paper towels for his oozing nose.

"Her name is Hannah. For god's sake, her name is Hannah Ziebarth, and Milo beat her up after he got her pregnant. Don't you care?"

"What I care about is holding this family together—

that's what I care about!" my father rages. "And I suggest"—his finger pokes at my chest—"that you do the same! Do you understand, young man?"

I shove his finger away. "No, you're wrong. Our family can't come first all the time. We can't just . . ." Words don't come easily—if I could just write it. "We can't just throw people aside. We can't—"

"I have offered to pay the girl," he yells.

"Why not make Milo pay?" At last it comes out right. "Why not make him go to work and pay out of his own money? He put Hannah in the hospital—twice. Make him pay some of it."

"That's ridiculous," my father says. "Milo's going to Harvard, not working some piddling job to pay for a girl who doesn't have the sense to take care of herself!" His face is almost as red as the sweatshirt he's wearing. "Haven't you learned anything in this family?"

His question is so sad, and so is the answer. I can't talk anymore because I'm crying. My father, softening, puts his arm around me. "We want good things for you too, Son . . . ," he says. "Good school, great golf." He tightens his grip. "Isn't that right, Tiger Woods?"

I cry. Snot and tears cover my face, and I can't control the sobs. The sound of my father's voice, kind and intimate, makes me want to wail, because I know now that I will never like or respect him again, the same with my mother and Milo. I cry, because my unasked question isolates me so completely: What about being a good person?

The next day the doctor says Milo's nose is broken.

Two weeks into winter semester, Hannah comes back to school. I see her at a distance in the morning at her locker with her friends, Trilby Evans and Hilary Watson. Her hair is shorter, and she doesn't laugh out loud with them. They giggle and snort the way girls do, but she just smiles with them. At lunch I see her across the lunchroom. Kids come up to her and ask her how she is. Again it seems to me that Hannah isn't as quick to laugh as she used to be. Maybe I'm reading into it.

I don't see her close up until last period when she walks into Mr. Krauss's American history class with Trilby Evans, who hovers near her like a mother-protectress. Hannah wears a new sweater, the same color blue as her eyes. Trilby sits down reluctantly while Hannah hands her late registration slip to Mr. Krauss, who signs it and welcomes her back, his bow tie flitting up and down when he speaks. Kids call him the Talking Tie.

I sit in the back, and she doesn't notice me until the Talking Tie asks her to take any available seat, and her eyes scan the classroom. When she does see me, she nods slightly, pressing her lips together. Her acknowledgment blows me away, and I stare at her, probably with my dumb mouth open.

The only seat in the class is one aisle over and in front of me. She's still as thin as she ever was, maybe thinner. You wouldn't know she had a baby a few weeks ago, although everybody *does* know. And everybody knows about the DNA test and why Milo is spending the rest of his senior year at Coronado Academy. Everyone knows as if the finger of God had written the whole account on the walls in the main hall.

I've waited two weeks to see Hannah, and now that she's back I don't know what I expect. It's not like we're going to be friends. Still, I'm excited that she'll be sitting in front of me the rest of the year, where I can watch her fingers twist her hair while she takes notes. Maybe I've been waiting for that slight tilt of the head, that nod, that says she knows I'm not like Milo. It'll have to be enough.

After class, she and Trilby leave together, and a few minutes later I see them down the hall at Hilary Watson's locker chortling together like birds on a wire.

I make sure my chemistry book is in my backpack and head out the front door and up the hill to the parking lot. I can feel the sun on my back, thanks to a January thaw. Even the 4Runner is warm inside, and I roll down the front windows and toss my parka into the backseat. If the thaw continues, the remaining snow will be gone by the weekend, and I can play golf at Nibley. I start the engine and pull out into a long row of cars slowly making their way out of the parking lot.

Then I see Hannah, pulling her flute case out of a tan Prizm and locking the door. She's to the right of me and she stands in back of the Prizm, her hand shielding her eyes from the afternoon sun as she waits for cars to pass so she can cross the parking lot. It startles her to see me in the 4Runner, but she recovers quickly. I stop and signal her to cross in front of me.

She does but surprises me by coming around to the

open window. "I forgot my flute," she says, a little breathless. She stands back from the door and looks down the row of cars in front of me to see if she's holding me up, but the parking lot is now plugged tight.

As usual, I can't think of a thing to say except "Hi," which seems pretty lame.

"Well," she says, taking a deep breath. There's the tiniest scar above one eye. She looks down the row of cars again.

I try my best to smile a little so she doesn't mistake my silence for hostility. Finally I say her name, "Hannah—"

At the same time, she says mine, "Roman—"

Then we both laugh. "What were you going to say?" she asks.

I shake my head. "Nothing, I . . ." What *can* I say?

Her face is in the window now, her hands grasping the door. "You came to the hospital, didn't you?" Her eyes, unflinching, look directly into mine. She won't accept anything but the truth.

"How did you know?" I ask.

"The nurse—"

"I didn't tell her my name—"

"She said a boy came to see the baby, a tall, thin boy, wearing a T-shirt that had 'St. George Amateur Golf Classic' on the front of it." She smiles. "I knew it was you."

I nod.

"Did you like him?" She has to press her lips together after she asks this question.

"I liked him a lot." My voice is gravelly and I turn

and see that my knuckles are white from clutching the steering wheel too tightly. I look back at her. "He smiled at me," I say.

Little shudders of air escape her lips and she tries to smile. "He was beautiful, wasn't he?"

"Yes," I say. "He was very beautiful."

Her smile wobbles. "Thanks, Roman," she whispers.

I nod.

She backs away from the window, but our eyes stay focused on each other for a few more seconds.

Then we look away.

"Well," she says, her voice light again. "I have arpeggios to play."

"Toot your flute," I say.

"See ya tomorrow." She waves and sprints around parked cars and down the hill.

Hannah Ziebarth. What I can't tell you is how I wish we could have kept him for all of us: for you and Milo and Tony and Gina and Rose. For my parents and your mother. What I can't tell you is that I, like you, will spend the rest of my life looking for a handsome boy with wide-set eyes and a dimpled smile.

Uncles have no rights.

PART V

Hannah Speaks

I don't know when I first realized that I would not—could not—keep my baby. Maybe it was when Trilby sat across from me at the Burger Bar, stunned that I would even consider not finishing high school. Maybe it was working full-time there instead of going to school fall semester and experiencing the awful dreariness of the work. Maybe it was the physics class I took at night at the community college and hearing Mr. Ketchum lecture on the string theory of the universe. It was like poetry. And when I tried to explain it to Bliss the next day, she said, "Thank god, I don't have to learn that crapload of stuff for a fast-food career."

Maybe it was that call to Rosmarin after I got home when she railed on me again that, "No matter what," I should never give in to the adults. "It's *your* life and *your* baby." Her words slurred together. It's the baby's life too, I had thought. And isn't the whole point finally to become an adult? Isn't that the point?

Maybe it was seeing that other baby with his parents at the Gallivan Center that night, the way when one parent got tired, the other took him, or when the baby grew bored with one, he moved to the other. It was a natural dance for three.

Maybe it was seeing that book full of couples aching for a baby.

Maybe it was that Mama and I were both getting a better sense of ourselves together and apart and learning to be happy without Daddy. I did not want to disturb that delicate and hard-won gift.

At the last moment when I saw him and held him and smelled the intoxicating, newborn scent of him, I was tempted to change my mind and rush him home with me. Maybe it was Milo himself who kept me from doing so. When he had to admit he was the father, I no longer had to be the liar/whore skulking around my own community. I could return to high school.

Maybe in the end, it was that no one forced me to give him up—not Mama, not Caitlin, not Rosa Benson, not the bishop. The decision was wholly mine.

It is Memorial Day and Mama and I are in the backyard cutting roses for a large bouquet to put on Daddy's grave. She has wrapped a Crisco can in foil and taped a brick of wet Oasis in the can so the stems will stand upright.

"I don't think the roses ever looked better," she says, snipping a perfect bloom. "What's this called?" She holds it up.

I look up at the pale pink blossom with the darker edges. "Perfecta," I say.

"Amazing. I don't know how you know one from another."

"The same way you know an orange jessamine from a crab apple." I add three stems of Mister Lincolns to the can.

Mama fits the Perfectas in. "We need some yellow ones and then we're done."

There are only two blooming Gold Crowns, and I pick them both and hand them to her. She can barely fit them into the crowded bouquet. "Glorious," she says, holding the can in both hands. She lifts her face to the sun and closes her eyes. "The whole day is glorious."

Seeing Mama outside and enjoying it is still new enough that I feel grateful. The layered shelves against the house are filled with bonsai and so is her worktable.

Mama hands the can of roses to me. "Maybe next year I'll be well enough to go to the cemetery with you."

"That'd be nice," I say. And it will be; although this year I'm kind of glad to be going alone, to sit in solitude next to Daddy's grave. "I better go," I say. "I want to be there early before all the crowds are there."

Mama nods. "I'm making Daddy's potato salad for lunch," she says. She walks along the side of the house with me down to the car, which is parked in front of the house. I put the roses on the passenger side in the front and walk around the car.

"You'll be careful, won't you?" Mama says, and I

have to remember that everybody's mother says that, not just my anxious mama.

"I'll be careful. I've been driving for almost a year now!" It's intended to make her feel better.

She laughs then. "But you've only been sixteen for nine months! Some comfort." She waves me off and walks up the stairs to the porch.

I honk and drive away.

Even though it's only a little after seven o'clock, the cemetery is filled with other early risers and already looks cheerful with flowers in cans, in vases, and on wreaths. Daddy's grave is on the northeast side of the cemetery and not hard to find, because it's close to where the soldiers are buried, and I can see the American flags flying one per grave long before I actually get there. He's buried near, not under, a willow tree. I like that tree. I stand in front of the gravestone—*Brian Wallace Ziebarth* etched into the gray marble—clutching the can of roses.

"Hi, Daddy," I whisper. "Long time no see." It feels like an epitaph. I stoop down and place the roses below his name and sit down on the grass next to them and with my fingers feel the letters in the stone. "Long time no see." Speaking aloud feels contrived, and so I think about what I'd say if I could talk with him. I think about Mama getting too anxious to do anything at all and my meeting Milo. I think about how I thought that if you loved someone deeply, they automatically loved you back.

I thought Milo would love me as much as you did,

Daddy. You taught me to love. Milo taught me to be cautious with my love.

I think about Bishop Kelsey helping me with the paternity suit and Rosa Benson telling me she would help with the baby if I wanted to keep it. I think of Trilby's family taking me to San Francisco with them over spring break and Caitlin Saunders's expressive brown eyes when she said, "You're working so hard. You've made an incredible recovery. Do you know that?" I think of Roman wanting to make sure I knew that he was not like his brother, that he was on my side.

I am loved, Daddy.

The baby. My baby. He is almost five months old. He must look different from the pictures I took in the hospital—the ones I keep in my bottom drawer under the old flute music. He must have more hair. And he can probably laugh out loud and grasp small toys and roll over. Not an hour goes by that I don't think about him. Not one hour.

Watch over my baby, Daddy. Watch over him. If you are there, watch over him. Are you there, Daddy?

Looking up, I see clouds in the distance rolling in. By afternoon it will rain. The idea makes me smile.

Not far off is a new grave covered with wreaths and large bouquets with ribbons that say "Dad" or "Brother" in gold lettering. The flowers are still fairly fresh. Dad and Brother must have been buried the day before.

People don't die in real life the way they do in the movies. They don't necessarily say smooth last words.

Their hands don't slip gently out of yours. But most of all, their eyes don't close. It is the one memory of Daddy that I would like to forget but can't. The way he lay on the floor, his eyes half shut, half open. Could he see us? Was he really dead? I had taken CPR, but when I tried to do it I wasn't sure I remembered it right. Did I breathe into him hard enough? Did I pinch his nostrils shut? Did I push down on the right part of his chest? Surely there was a magic word, a gesture, an act I could have performed that would have brought him back, made him leap to his feet, exclaiming, "That was a close one!" While all the other memories of him fade, that last one doesn't.

I stand up, hoping to shake off this thought. I wander down a gentle slope reading names: Katseanas, Hornes, Hebdons—a whole cluster of them—Wrights, Cannons, and McFarlands. I stop. Baby Roos. No first name. It is a white stone with a lamb sculpted above the name. Born March 1, 1952. Died March 3, 1952. Two days old. That was how old my baby was when I handed him over to the social worker. Baby Ziebarth.

I walk back up the slope and pull a pale Pink Blush from Daddy's bouquet and take it back down to Baby Roos and lay it on the stone.

"Hello, Hannah," someone calls to me. I turn, and it is Rosa walking across the narrow road. "I saw your car and thought you must be close by." She's dressed in new khaki slacks and a checkered shirt. She sees the rose and the dates and looks away quickly. "Harry is buried across the road from your father. I always bring them both a little something."

I nod and smile. "Nice," I say. It feels awkward to be caught in front of the baby's grave. "I—I found this sad grave. The baby's only two days old." I stop.

A little "Hmm" escapes her lips.

"It's nice to have a place—that is, an *official* place to mourn. I wish . . ." What exactly do I wish? That my baby had died so I'd have a place to grieve?

"I know what you mean," she says briskly. "We could all use a place to mourn for those people who have"—she hesitates—"not died, but who have gone out of our lives."

I nod my head. Yes, that's it. I'm grateful for her directness.

"Why don't you make such a place, Hannah? There's room behind your father's grave."

"You mean get a second gravestone?" Too weird.

She smiles. "I was thinking of something more modest. You could plant something—something like a rosebush. There's plenty of sun, and the grounds are watered every day."

"Like a memory garden." I like the idea.

"Yes."

"I've never planted a bush before—"

"It's not hard."

"Would you help?" I wouldn't have dared ask her such a question a year ago. "Or maybe it takes too much time—"

"We could do it this morning if you want."

"Really?" I am so excited, I clasp my hands together.

"Leave your car here and we'll take my Blazer." She is already walking toward the road, and I have to hustle to catch up with her.

We drive to a nursery behind Trolley Square that has hundreds of rosebushes. I have a hard time choosing, but I finally decide on a Pink Peace, which I know is hardy. It has one perfect opening bloom on it.

"Good choice," Rosa says.

I set the bush in a grocery cart and follow her to the cashier.

"We'll need some of this," she says, picking a can of rose food off the shelf.

I stop and check to see how much money I have. Only enough for the bush.

"The rose food is my treat. You go pay for the bush. I'll catch up in a minute."

"Gee, thanks." I push the cart in front of the register. After I've paid, I wheel the cart to Rosa's Blazer and put the rosebush in the back. Rosa, carrying a shopping bag, is leaving the store as I return the cart. "Let's stop by the house and get a shovel," she says.

When we get to her house, Mama is out in the front yard, weeding. It still surprises me to see her outside.

"You'd better tell your mother what we're doing so she doesn't worry," Rosa says. She heads up her walk and yells, "Hi, Nora," to Mama. I get out of the car and slowly close the door. Mama walks down the slope to meet me.

"Did you get in an accident?" she asks. The worry lines mark her forehead.

"Oh, no—nothing like that. I met Rosa up in the cemetery and—uh, I—I—we got this idea." I know I'm stammering. I want to lie to her. I just don't want to explain.

"But where's the car?" Always that anxiety in her face.

"It's still at the cemetery." I try to smile. "It's okay, Mama. Rosa and I are going to plant a rosebush behind Daddy's gravestone—like a memory garden."

Relief. "Oh, that's nice. He'll have roses blooming all summer." I want to let her think I am doing it for Daddy. I know she wants me to forget about the baby and get on with my life. I could just say, yes, Mama, the rose garden is for Daddy, and I wouldn't have to hear about forgetting the baby, which is impossible. Surely she must know that?

I shouldn't hide myself from Mama. Caitlin said that. She said I had to be myself and Mama had to be herself.

"Actually," I start, "we're planting a memory garden for—for my baby."

"But the baby isn't—"

"No, he isn't dead, but—I need a place where it's all right for me to mourn him."

Mama stares at me but doesn't speak. Maybe she's thinking of something Caitlin said to her. I don't know.

"I can't talk about him with my friends because it makes them uncomfortable." I say. "I can't talk about him with you because you're afraid I'll turn into a raving talking tree again."

She smiles and shakes her head. "I try not to think that," she says.

"I know. I'm okay, Mama. Honestly, I'm okay."

Rosa is coming along the side of her house now, carrying a shovel and a pick.

We both glance at her and turn back to each other. Mama grasps my shoulders. "I'm okay too," she says. "You don't have to worry about me either."

Rosa throws the shovel and the pick into the back of the Blazer. "We'll only be an hour or so," she says, slamming the door.

"Sounds fine," Mama says. To me she says, "It's a good idea, Hannah. I really think so."

At the cemetery Rosa shows me how to use the pick, and I pull up the grass and loosen the dirt behind Daddy's gravestone. She shovels the dirt into a pile. We work until we have a good-sized hole. Rosa shows me how to separate the roots and fill the dirt in around them. We do this with our hands.

I like the dirt. It reminds me of finger painting with chocolate pudding. "It feels good," I say.

"Nothing's better," Rosa says, patting the dirt down around the rosebush. "Gardeners go to heaven."

I look up when she mentions heaven. "Do you think there is such a place? I mean, do you think there's a life after death?"

"I hope so." Her fingers play with the dirt now.

"You're not sure?" I'm a little surprised, because Rosa is always going to church, and I assumed that she would be more knowing.

"I *hope*, Hannah. I don't *know* anything. No one comes back and tells you, do they?"

I shake my head. "No, they don't."

"Still, I hope there's more. Although I doubt any of us has the least notion of what that other existence is like." She sits back on her haunches and wipes the sweat off her forehead. "Sure would like to see Harry again, though—and my parents—a lot of people, actually."

"You know what I like about you?" I say.

She smirks as if waiting for me to be my usual smarty-party self.

"No, really," I say. "You don't talk crap."

She laughs then—a deep, masculine laugh. It's a laugh I like.

"You laugh like a smoker," I say, grinning at her.

"I've never smoked in my life!"

"Like Bette Davis. You sound like Bette Davis when you laugh."

"You're too young to know about Bette Davis," she says. She stands and stomps the dirt around the bush.

"I watch old movies. I know what she sounds like."

When she leans over to pick up the shovel and pick, she's still smiling. "You're a piece of work, Hannah." It sounds like a compliment.

Following her directions, I spread rose food under the bush. Then we stand and look at our work. "It looks great," I say. The one bloom stretches up to the sun.

"It needs one little touch." Rosa bends down and takes a smooth rock out of the bag from the nursery.

With both hands, she sets it down in front of the rosebush.

It isn't until she's standing again that I see a word
etched neatly into the rock. One word: *Baby.*

Rosa looks at my face and must see that I can't
speak. "A rose grows in his memory," she says.

I can only nod. Ah, weary wee flipperling, curl at thy
ease.

She picks up her tools and the empty shopping bag
and walks to her car.

I will have to thank her later.

ABOUT THE AUTHOR

Louise Plummer was born in the Netherlands and came to America with her parents when she was five years old. She and her husband, Tom, have lived in Cambridge, Massachusetts, and St. Paul, Minnesota. They now live in Salt Lake City, where she is an associate professor of English. Her most recent novel for Delacorte Press was *The Unlikely Romance of Kate Bjorkman.*

About *A Dance for Three,* Louise Plummer says, "I knew I would write about a teenage pregnancy when a close relative of mine became pregnant. I realized that the pregnancy itself was only part of a whole group of problems; so with fifteen-year-old Hannah Ziebarth, I wanted to show how a pregnancy affects a girl who is already overwhelmed with a troubled life."